CENTRAL PASSAGE

LAWRENCE SCHOONOVER

CENTRAL PASSAGE

WILLIAM SLOANE ASSOCIATES · NEW YORK

To:
SARA SCHOONOVER
with Admiration, Respect and a Love
that has flowered over a
Lifetime
this book is affectionately
Dedicated

Contents

PART ONE

THE
TWENTY MINUTE
WAR

CHAPTER 1

IT'S been done since the days of the Neanderthal man, she thought to herself, and to a degree it was a consolation. If it hadn't I suppose none of us would be here at all.

When she first began to appear in the supermarket in loose blouses the women who were Bill's and her friends looked at her curiously, averting their eyes and holding their tongues for a while. Then one of them came right out with it and said, "Betty, you're getting prettier every day! I wish I had a complexion like yours, so delicate!" And the woman looked at her knowingly.

Most of their friends already had children and could spot the early signs like hawks.

"I certainly haven't felt blooming," she said.

The woman said, "When is it going to be?"

Betty said, "Oh, the doctor says it'll be pretty soon now," and blushed.

"We'll give you a great big christening party," the woman said amiably. "Honestly, Betty, you should have let me in on the secret. I could have done your shopping for you when

3

you didn't feel quite tiptop. Sometimes girls don't with their first, you know. I know I didn't."

Betty reflected that that must have been a long time ago. Her friend already had three, and the oldest was almost ready for high school.

There was certainly nothing shameful in a young married woman's first pregnancy, but Betty was old-fashioned about the matter and a little shy.

Sometimes she reflected upon the little she remembered from the history courses she had taken in school: history seemed one long recitation of wars, whole populations engulfed in slaughter and bloodshed, ancient cities besieged and conquered, Biblical nomads in tents wandering in wildernesses and always kings "smiting"—in the Bible they were always "smiting"—each other with the edge of the sword, slaying their enemies in battle by the thousands and thousands of thousands. Where were the pregnant women in those far-off heroic days? And yet, Betty mused, there must have been long periods of quiet, peace and security, for otherwise the women would never have borne the children who constituted the ancestors of all mankind. So not all of history could have been violent.

Violent too was the animal world, if one were to believe the biology books, big fish eating little fish, cats scratching, dogs fighting, often to the death—and yet the world was full of cats and dogs and fish. So they too, in the animal world, managed to find peaceful interludes in which to increase and multiply.

At any rate, this was the only answer Betty could find in the puzzle of the history she had studied in school, a history, she decided, that recorded only the highlights, the dramatic boastful stories of battle and death.

Patently, history was written by men, not by women,

especially not by women in the tedious, patient, uncomfortable process of carrying their young.

Her pregnancy had been very uncomfortable. She had expected nausea and morning sickness for the first three
months, since three months was the time that all the books
said it would last, and all her friends when they spoke of
their own pregnancies had seemed to agree on three months;
but Betty's had persisted up to the present time, very near
the end, until four o'clock in the afternoon, and it worried
her considerably.

"There isn't any pattern," the doctor at the Base had said.
"Especially with the first one. You are perfectly normal.
Next time it will be smooth sailing."

Betty hoped he was right, though how a Navy doctor, a
bachelor with twenty-nine years' service on Navy vessels
where women were nonexistent, a doctor due for retirement
next year, could have had much experience delivering babies
Betty simply could not imagine.

Bill had laughed heartily at that, but he was never rough
with her. "Innocent." He chuckled. "Innocent, that's what
you are. Navy doctors have been delivering babies for years.
Do you think *all* they do is patch up cuts and set broken legs
when sailors fall down hatches, and dole out the blue ointment?"

"Blue ointment?"

Bill felt he had gone too far.

"Bill, what is blue ointment?"

"Well, it isn't for married men," he said.

"If you don't tell me I'll ask one of the girls."

"Heck, they wouldn't know. I hope. If they did, they
wouldn't tell you."

She looked alarmed, so he told her, feeling a little embarrassed; and she said, "How filthy."

"Mostly," Bill said, changing the subject, "Navy doctors are just about like any doctors, with the same practice as the rest of them. They cut out appendixes and give you cold shots and pills so your kids don't get polio *and* they deliver babies, better than most doctors, cleaner, quicker, and they knock you out so you don't feel anything. Civilian doctors like to give the mother a hard time. Not Navy doctors. They've all had war experience and they know what pain is."

Bill had absolute faith in everything Naval, and if Bill had, so had Betty. Moreover, Bill was usually right about practical things. When the sink clogged he could "free" it, as he expressed the process, with an ingeniously bent coat hanger, the wire things that the tailor gave you free when he delivered your clothes. "No use calling a six-dollar-an-hour plumber for that," he would say cheerfully. And when she would start to kiss him in recognition of his genius he would say, "Just a minute, honey; I'm all dirty." And when he had washed his hands, while the sink emptied like a whirlpool, he would hug her and say, "Wouldn't want a plumber in here when I'm not here, anyhow. You're too cute."

He was big and slow and tender and cheerfully aware that lots of people were smarter than he, but he was jealous of nobody and sometimes he would say, shrugging ruefully, "Betty, I bet when I've got about thirty years' service under my belt they'll give me a commission. On the day I retire I'll probably get my first and last salute."

"Bill, it'll be lots sooner than that."

"Well, if it isn't nobody's going to starve. I can't lose my job, like civilians do."

He was thorough; he was competent; he was quite right, she knew, about not losing his job. He would advance and advance in the service.

"For an eighth-grade education I haven't done too badly,"

he said, frowning almost apologetically. "I've studied hard at my job."

He wanted to believe she was right: that he would get a commission sooner than he expected. But there were so many smart young ensigns flooding into the service these days. Annapolis was graduating more than ever before, the academy having doubled in size, all those ensigns, them and their rings. He was not jealous, but he regretted just missing the enlargement of the academy. The ensigns were only a year or so younger than he. If he had been born a year or two or three later he too might have qualified for the enlarged academy, he too might have been an ensign with a ring, and Betty would then be an officer's wife, and the baby she carried would have a legacy in the academy. Heck. It hadn't happened.

Betty saw his thoughtful face.

"We will call him Wilson Young, Jr.," she said, smiling. "That will keep people from mixing him up with Wilson Young, Sr., the Admiral."

She could smile without effort now, for it was evening and her morning sickness had finally passed and she could take nourishment without immediately losing it.

Bill grinned. She was better educated than he, but she did not feel superior; sometimes, especially since her pregnancy, she felt humble. That was what love had done to Betty Young, and she was glad it had.

"You seem pretty sure it'll be a boy," he said cautiously.

"We both want a boy, so it will be a boy."

"I'd love a girl, too," he said earnestly. "Even a girl."

"*Even!*" She laughed. "Oh, Bill, you never could hide how you feel."

"Why should I? But I mean it, Betty, I'd sure love a cute

little girl. They're awful cute. Probably like you when you were little. Lots of fathers have girls."

"Dear Bill!" she said, hugging him. "Dear, dear Bill. Never mind. It'll be a boy. I promise."

"Well, if it is," he said, "can't we name him 'William' instead of 'Wilson'? I've tried to hide that 'Wilson' all my life. Sure, I was named for the president, but I'll never be president and anyhow, we don't have to start a 'Wilson' tradition in the Young family."

Betty said, "He will be named for the grandest, sweetest, most wonderful man in the world, and that's you. That's that."

"I don't know how I got you," he said in such honest bewilderment that she kissed him, suddenly, hotly, unexpectedly. The reaction of his big arms, copper-tanned by the Panama sun, was instinctive: his hug hurt her ribs and pressed her end-of-term figure strongly against him, and she winced away.

"Oh gosh," he said, repentant. "I shouldn't have done that."

She said, laughing, "I don't think you did any damage. Maybe it'll hurry things up."

Bill pondered the thought that women were strange and wonderful things, something you put on a pedestal if they were mothers or sisters or wives. Of course there was the other kind—there were only two kinds, a cleavage sharp as those who saluted and those who were saluted—the kind you could say anything to and do anything with, when you were a bachelor and got drunk in foreign ports. But later you put all that behind you and saved your petty officer's pay against the time when you took a wife and became a brown-bagger, for there was dignity even in that, and you even tried to put a little aside for the luxuries you wanted to buy her. The government allowance was never enough for all you wanted to do for a wife. He remembered with anger the time when something about the "dollar deficiency" had sent thousands of wives and children back to the States while their husbands and fathers remained on bases abroad. There had been such an uproar, such a falling off of enlistments—even ensigns wanted out, them and their rings, stating that they would never make the Navy a career—that the policy had been quickly reversed. But still the government allowances were never all they ought to be. Yes, a man had to take care of his women; half the time they didn't know what was happening, real vague and discontented. And yet women could be strangely direct in things they understood thoroughly in their personal feminine world, and say things like, "Maybe it'll hurry things up." Bill could never have made such a remark. Even if he had thought of it he would have said it some other way.

He certainly would never have given her that bear hug to bring it about. He had treated her as if she were made of glass ever since that night when, in bed, she had whispered that a baby was on the way.

I think he's a little old-fashioned, Betty thought fondly. Perhaps that was what made a gentleman, to be absolutely normal and a little old-fashioned. She basked in his warmth and tenderness, for she knew that, despite her somewhat better education, she was very, very much like him. Not by any means that they shared each other's specialized knowledge. The women's magazines always had articles about how you should take an interest in your partners' jobs, the wife in the husband's, the husband in the wife's. Now what would Bill be good for in a supermarket, and what good would she be in a ship's bilge if a pump went wrong? She would not even be able to talk intelligently about such a thing. And the thought of Bill in an apron whipping up a tasty snack in the kitchen made her laugh, in a shuddery fashion. No; such "sharing," as it was called, was not for Bill or Betty Young. It was better to be just what they were, each good at his own job, each respecting the other's job—but letting the other do it. That was "sharing" in a broader sense, and if it wasn't it ought to be. I guess I'm just about average, she thought, making no apologies.

Average the baby no doubt would be also, and surely that was for the best. Geniuses never had any friends, and lived alone, and nobody but other geniuses knew what they were talking about. What a lonesome world it would be if everyone were a genius!

These comfortable bourgeois ruminations of Bill and Betty Young took place before The Twenty Minute War.

But not very long before.

CHAPTER 2

SOCIOLOGISTS have a tendency nowadays, especially the younger ones, to smile amusedly at the refusal of several large nations to send exhibits to the 1964 World's Fair in New York City, citing this reluctance as a typical manifestation of the absurd nationalism that gripped the world at that time and the tragic preoccupation with trivia that seemed to exert a hypnotic sway over the minds of political leaders. But this is hindsight, inevitable perhaps in the wake of all the great events that followed. At the time, the reluctance to exhibit at a World's Fair was deemed ominous. The excuses were deemed specious. One nation pleaded a prior commitment, one protested that the World's Fair did not represent the whole world and hence was illegal, and one refused sulkily on the ground that the invitation to exhibit had been tendered verbally instead of via the ambassadorial pouch with due ceremony. The truth seems to be that the nations with anything to exhibit did not wish to exhibit, lest they divulge the secret giant strides they had made in the science of the atom.

In the end, of course, prodded by newspaper speculation

that came very near to the truth, they all agreed to exhibit, but privately determined to suppress all publicity of their awesome atomic progress and to feature only such peaceful arts as were useful for propaganda purposes and which no spy would bother to steal. Even this limited area of understanding, in the current atmosphere of suspicion, was difficult of achievement and required much coming and going of delegations.

At Washington Municipal Airport, surrounded by TV cameras and news correspondents with portable tape recorders, Academician Anapolskoi boarded the Russian jet liner that would take the Soviet Cultural Delegates back to Moscow. It was a sleek, delta-winged craft with its jets farther aft than was common in American planes, and there was only one engine, a fact that bespoke the Russians' supreme confidence in its reliability and thrust. The delegation had completed its work, all arrangements were made for Soviet participation in the Fair, and the press of America had assembled to bid them a cordial farewell.

Academician Anapolskoi was last in the order of precedence up the long ramp, being only a passenger. He was not an official member of the delegation. He was not interviewed, since he would not preside over an exhibition of tractors or conduct an orchestra or score a ballet or engage in any of the other cultural activities of the forthcoming Soviet exhibit.

He was human enough to wish that one of the American newsmen had asked him to record his views on his own specialty, which was oceanography. He was a long-time friend of Emperor Hirohito and he had known the old Prince Albert the First of Monaco. But the Emperor's contribution to marine science had been forgotten in Japan's defeat after World War II; and as for Prince Albert of Monaco, he was commonly confused with an old-fashioned type of coat and a smoking tobacco. The only Monegasques now known to Americans were Prince Rainier and Princess Grace, who were more "photogenic," as the word went in America. In American English "photogenic" meant "pretty in pictures" or "eminently photographable." In Greek, which was closer to the Russian, it meant "born of the light."

That made the old academician smile. "Born of the light, indeed!" No one but an empty-headed reader of the American movie magazines would pay that pleasant harmless couple so cosmic an accolade, whereas the Great Ones, like Albert and Hirohito, they were forgotten, as forgotten as Academician Anapolskoi. And yet, in justice, he thought that if the empty-headed masses of all countries, America especially, chose to idealize beauty and youth and love and romance, there was still good grounds, biological grounds, for hope in the future for this shrinking, suspicious, satellite-girdled world. I am of course a little out of date, he admitted to himself. But so was Boris Pasternak, whom I admired. But Pasternak was a poet, and he talked too much, and they crucified him. It occurred to Anapolskoi that "crucified" was a term out of favor at home. But they respect my science and they have praised my charts, and it is not necessary for an oceanographer to talk politics.

It would have been pleasant if at least one of the American newsmen had tried to interview him.

But no, I am not jealous of the Director of the Bolshoi Ballet, Academician Anapolskoi assured himself, as the Director, after a long videotaped interview, proceeded him up the ramp, to considerable applause from the American spectators.

Dancing, thought Academician Anapolskoi, is something I too enjoy, at least when the music has rhythm. There is a purpose in rhythm. There is rhythm in the heartbeat, rhythm in the seasons, and above all rhythm in the tides, and all are purposeful and allied to Life.

The Bolshoi Ballet danced to rhythm; rhythm was also in their sinuous gliding, their leaping, their posturing, like salmon leaping the waterfalls in their migrations upstream to the fresh waters of their birth, like birds trumpeting and strutting before their mates in the mating season. These rhythms had biological purpose and hence were beautiful and hence were good.

American music, on the other hand, seemed to have no rhythm. It grunted and wailed and the lyrics made nonsense. Academician Anapolskoi agreed with his sociological colleagues that American music was symptomatic of degeneracy. But he had heard the Bolshoi Director state during his television interview that something new was creeping into American popular songs, even into the jingling commercials on the radio; that new note was a martial drum beat like an old-fashioned rally to arms. The Director had meant it as a compliment, but Anapolskoi knew that the chance remark would be soberly evaluated by the Russian military men when the Director made his cultural report to Moscow.

No, Academician Anapolskoi was not jealous of the limelight. It was only natural that these young American newsmen should be more interested in the pectoral and pygal measurements of the prima ballerina, amply described by the Bolshoi Director and evoking good-natured whistles of amazement because they were given in centimeters, than in the fascinating geophysical fact that the Gulf Stream splits into three currents before it reaches Europe and then it returns to Panama. The Gulf Stream had behaved in this fashion for some hundreds of thousands of years. Its exquisitely beautiful transatlantic course could hardly be considered news, despite its beneficent result on the race, despite the very great likelihood that without it there would be no race at all, or at least no prima ballerina.

Academician Anapolskoi had just been to Panama in the further pursuance of his research. How careless the Americans were, he mused, to permit him, a scientist, free run of the Canal installation. How infinitely more circumspect his own countrymen with the new Don-Volga Canal! He considered himself lucky to have been permitted a visa. Why, I might have been a spy! he thought. But they probably realized I haven't the interest, I'm not the type; there are Russians better qualified.

In fact, he considered himself lucky to be alive at all. Ironically, he owed his continued existence to a chance remark of Winston Churchill's in 1943.

"England is a sea animal," Churchill had said to Stalin. "Russia is a land animal."

Stalin had taken this as a reproach. In his vaulting ambition he was determined to be a better animal than England. He took the blue pencil that he always carried in the right breast pocket of his tunic and through the name of Andrei Yussopoff Anapolskoi, an intellectual fated for liquidation, scion of a princely house under the Czar, he drew a thick blue line, for Anapolskoi was Russia's most gifted oceanographer. Russia would need such men, noble blood or no, if Russia were to become a sea animal like England. A heavy dossier, subsequently compiled, minutely screened and searchingly evaluated, revealed that Anapolskoi was not in the least politically minded. He was saved to make charts of ocean currents for the ever-growing secret fleet of Soviet submarines.

When Stalin died Anapolskoi was left in peace to pursue his studies and draw up his nautical charts, which proved so amazingly accurate that the Russian Navy preferred them to the British, hitherto the best in the world. Soviet Intelligence had always laid hands on these British charts and distributed them so efficiently that the Russian commanders often had them before the admirals of the Royal Navy. Now Anapolskoi's superseded them.

Shortly he was elected to the Soviet Academy of Sciences, a coveted position that entitled him to be called "Academician" in ordinary discourse instead of "Comrade." An Academician was also entitled to benefits of a more substantial kind. Like workers who exceeded their quota he was rewarded by a higher standard of living. He was given a larger apartment in crowded Moscow and a state salary that, in buying power, was far above a comparable professor's in England or America. Russia paid her intellectuals well if they could launch a space vehicle, concoct a fuel with a heavier thrust, or trace an ocean current for the benefit of her Navy. And if in their free time they chose to indulge themselves in harmless basic research they were not forbidden, not even if they made two-headed dogs, provided always they possessed the energy, and turned their notes over to the local scientific committee. One never knew when some bit of apparently useless research might prove very useful indeed, either for propaganda purposes in the political sphere or coupled with and complementing some other bit of knowledge dredged up out of some other thinker's compulsion to delve into the curious, the impractical, the esoteric. It was important to keep geniuses happy, for otherwise, inexplicably, they ceased to be geniuses. Academician Anapolskoi was therefore as well off, or better off, in Russia than anywhere else in the world, and he was a happy man.

The big delta-winged craft rose sharply into the sky, leaving behind a smokeless trail of shimmering heat that engulfed the Washington Municipal Airport like the crack of doom. More than one American military man thought to himself, I would like to get my hands on an ounce, even half an ounce, of that fuel. But though newsmen had been invited to inspect the luxurious interior of the airliner, stern-faced guards with lumps under their tunics and hands-in-breast like Napoleon, obviously fingering the triggers of pistols, had kept them away from the cockpit and the engine.

When the plane disappeared, American technicians scraped the scorched cement of the runway. They were dressed as ordinary laborers and it looked as if they were simply inspecting the scorched spots for bits of cement that might have become loosened under the intense heat and that might be sucked into the intakes of jet engines and cause trouble. But they were all trained technicians and they were looking for the secret of the Russian jet fuel. In the laboratory, when the samples were analyzed, they found traces of aluminum. But how this metal, which had been used to make hotter everything from Thermite, a welding compound, to solid fuels for rockets, had been transformed by Russian science into a liquid that would neither clog nor corrode the Russian jet engine, posed a problem that seemed to require long study. The best guess was that aluminum had somehow been made to combine with an organic compound. This was frustrating because, of course, the organic molecules were destroyed in the process of combustion. But there was no doubt that the Russian plane took off and soared upward with unprecedented grace and speed.

Inside, in the middle seat, with another passenger, a satellite Deputy Premier, on his right by the window, and a musician on the aisle, Academician Anapolskoi leaned forward, looked out and saw the Washington Monument, needle-sharp and pigeon-stained, drop swiftly away and sail off on the ground as the aircraft left Washington behind.

"*Ectopistes migrarius* would never have roosted so high," muttered Academician Anapolskoi idly. "The last specimen of that intelligent breed died in 1914. Along with much else, so very much else," he sighed. He always equated the beginning of World War I with the death of his class, his noble family, his Czar, and the mighty changes that had come upon his beloved homeland. It was difficult to have outlived one world and lived into another, the future of which one could not foresee.

The satellite Deputy Premier took the murmured remark as an invitation to conversation.

"That overgrown obelisk was erected to honor George Washington," he said, flashing at it a malevolent smile of small, even teeth, startlingly white against his slightly gold-tinged complexion. "Once these Americans were a revolutionary people too." He said it with the defiant air of a schoolboy who has mastered his lesson and hurls the correct answer back at the teacher.

Academician Anapolskoi mused, "They made their nests in Patagonia as I remember. A remarkable breed."

"Who did?"

"I beg your pardon?" Anapolskoi said.

The Deputy Premier introduced himself with a florid enumeration of his titles. Anapolskoi identified himself modestly as an oceanographer, a fellow supercargo on the cultural mission plane.

"Whom did you call a remarkable breed, Comrade Anapolskoi?"

"Why, the *Ectopistes migrarius*. Pigeons."

"I was speaking of the American revolutionaries," said the satellite Deputy Premier.

"All dead now," Anapolskoi mused. "But they were wonderful birds."

The Deputy Premier's eyes narrowed and glinted. The epicanthic fold of his eyelids, all but bred out of his mixed blood, was discernible at such times. A threat leapt to his tongue but remained unspoken: So, too, soon, will the wicked capitalist imperialist Americans be dead! Instead he said smoothly, "Perhaps you did not hear me. I repeat, I was speaking of the American revolutionaries."

"Oh yes, I heard you. It is easy to hear on these new planes," Anapolskoi said.

The huge jet craft was now streaking through the sky well above the speed of sound. People on the ground heard the blast of the jet as a high-pitched scream as it entered its steep takeoff but to those inside the luxurious cabin all that was audible was a muted drone like the cellos pitched low in Tchaikovsky's *1812 Overture* just before the military trumpets blast forth their clarion call to arms and to death. Academician Anapolskoi wondered whether the Ballet Director was listening.

"Yes," Anapolskoi continued, "they revolted. But they're still the same breed, and under their softness and carelessness I suspect they're still fond of their same old revolutionary ideals. They helped Russia considerably against Hitler."

"Precisely," said the satellite Deputy Premier unpleasantly. "That is why they must be extinguished. Nothing must stand in the way of the onward march, the inevitable victory of our universal socialization everywhere in the world." He stressed the *our*.

Anapolskoi looked dubious. He rather disliked the intense little man. "I'm afraid sociology is quite out of my specialty, my Transylvanian friend," he said blandly.

The Deputy Premier winced at being called a Transylvanian, but he sensed that the Academician wished to avoid politics and reasoned that therefore he must be better informed than he pretended. He sucked in his breath and smiled ingratiatingly. "Tell me," he said, "tell me something that is in your own special sphere. I have always wondered. How did it happen, why did it come about, that the dinosaurs all perished at once? You will observe that though I am only a politician I am not totally uninstructed. All over the world we find their eggs, fertilized but unbroken, the embryos inside. They never hatched. No progenitors remain. No progeny resulted. Total, instantaneous extinction, all in a day. One day the dinosaurs were lords of creation, and the next day—nothing. They were all dead."

Anapolskoi shrugged. "I was always under the impression that the brutes in question developed bulk at the expense of their brains. Massive bodies, atrophied reasoning powers. You might use the American expression: they got too big for their britches. Or again, and much likelier, it might have been some sudden hostile climatic change."

"No," said the Deputy Premier, "it was a change of political climate. Dinosaur doomed himself because he was an individualist. He wallowed in his swamp and got lazy and fat and thought only about his own precious reptilian self and never gave a thought to his neighbors. Reptiles succumbed because primates took over dominion of the world, and we primates are socialized animals. On one great day of victory we primates arose in our might and eliminated the sluggards. It was the prehistoric analogue of the political change that is taking place right now, this very instant!"

Anapolskoi glanced distastefully at the satellite Deputy Premier, whose paleontology was some millions of years out of sequence and whose thesis was hardly worth considering. He disliked him not only for his ignorance but also because his name had a Tartar ring, Karajan Chanuris, and his faintly golden skin and suggestive eye-fold bespoke the trace of Oriental blood. Anapolskoi's noble Russian ancestors had slaughtered the Deputy Premier's ancestors by the hundreds of thousands, and conquered and civilized the remnant. But these descendants of the barbarians now set themselves up as more Russian than the Russians and more sovietized than the Soviets. Karajan Chanuris exhibited the characteristic zeal of the convert, which either amuses or nauseates the orthodox and is instantly detectable.

"I suppose all hypotheses are worth examining," Anapolskoi said noncommittally.

The Deputy Premier for his part was a bit contemptuous of Academician Anapolskoi, who kept forgetting that his country was no longer called "Transylvania" but on the contrary had achieved the status of a full-fledged People's Republic within the orbit of the USSR and possessed a respectable seacoast along the Black Sea.

Deputy Premier Karajan Chanuris was irked because, so far, the giant USSR had refused nuclear weapons to him and his Balkan colleagues, much as the USA had refused to share the secret of the atom and hydrogen bombs with her allies in the West. Such refusals, he felt, reduced one's friends to the status of second-class citizens, children who could not be trusted with anything sharp.

But since Academician Anapolskoi chose to be nonpolitically minded, Deputy Premier Karajan Chanuris steered the conversation into a channel calculated to loosen the old Russian intellectual's tongue.

"The Nicaragua Canal would have been much better for the Americans," he suggested.

Instantly Anapolskoi pricked up his ears. "Of course!" he agreed heartily. "The Americans should have dug through

Nicaragua instead of building all those locks and cutting through all those mountains in Panama. A sea-level channel is always better." He expatiated at some length about the relatively minor difficulties posed by the difference in height and timing between the Pacific and the Atlantic tides on the east and west coasts of the isthmus, which bored the Deputy Premier.

"Militarily better, too," interjected Karajan Chanuris. "A single bomb could knock out the Panama Canal."

"They know that now," Anapolskoi said. "Recently I saw the abandoned remains of a parallel cut across Panama. The Americans realized it was within reach of the bomb and stopped building it. They have also abandoned the Panama Air Base, except for a few maintenance personnel, knowing that airplanes cannot shoot down missiles."

"That is most gratifying," said the Deputy Premier.

"I take it as a sign that political tensions are easing," Anapolskoi said. "It is, as you say, most gratifying."

It was tedious, but never unfruitful, for a politician to chat with a scholar. A scholar viewed the world from a different point of view and sometimes foresaw currents in human behavior that a politician, with his harder, more realistic brain, could put to good use. Roosevelt had had his Professor Einstein; Churchill, his Professor Lindemann.

The Deputy Premier suggested brightly, "Do you not find it odd, Academician Anapolskoi, that the Americans refuse to deal with Mao Tse Tung, when they tolerate dictators in Portugal, Spain, Central America, to say nothing of their own Caribbean?"

Karajan Chanuris had used the wrong word.

"Toleration isn't so bad, my Transylvanian friend," Anapolskoi replied amiably, anachronistically. "If the emergent mammals had tolerated poor dinosaur I dare say we'd have a happier world today."

The Deputy Premier said, "I will never get you out of the Jurassic Age, Academician Anapolskoi."

"I really don't see why you should try."

Chanuris said with some heat, "Because I live in the world of today, and because the capitalistic imperialist warmongering Americans threaten us with extinction and have ringed us round with nuclear bases and posted nuclear submarines in our waters and because you, Academician Anapolskoi, you and your Russians, refuse to arm us, your good friends, with bombs for our own preservation, which is inextricably linked with your own."

"I'm afraid I don't know a thing about all that," Anapolskoi said.

"Oh yes you do, and you have influence."

"You had better talk to the Presidium," Anapolskoi said. "I am, as you say, Jurassic. Weapons are not my specialty."

"But you know about them." There was no shaking the man.

Anapolskoi shrugged and answered, "Only what everyone knows. The Hiroshima bomb was a crude affair. Its energy yield was minimal. It 'smoked,' as it were, as did fifteenth-century gunpowder owing to incomplete combustion. In that bomb only a fraction of a fraction of one per cent of the energy in the classic Einsteinian formula, $E = mc^2$ was achieved. All the rest was cruel and dirty fallout, life-destroying nuclear 'smoke.' I remember when I was a boy, how I used to look at the chimneys of the huts of my father's serfs in the wintertime. How often I used to say to myself, 'Behold! There goes nine-tenths of the poor creature's firewood up in smoke. It neither warms the man nor gives heat for the wife's cooking. Pure waste.' In perfect bombs, of course, there will be no fallout.

"Later, with hydrogen fusion, the Americans improved their bombs. They smoked less. But still they smoked a little. That is all I know about the American bombs, though presumably Intelligence is better informed of their progress, if any. We, of course, have gone far beyond such primitive stages, as you know."

The Deputy Premier did not know, and his interest had reached a point of intensity where it took all his considerable power of dissimulation to keep it out of his face. He succeeded in maintaining a flat, impassive countenance and said in a controlled voice, "Of course, I know, Academician Anapolskoi; and naturally Russia is left with a glut of obsolete smoky bombs." He was guessing, but you could not tell he was guessing.

Anapolskoi nodded, unaware that he was betraying a closely kept secret. "Oh yes, that would follow inevitably. But I shouldn't imagine they'd have to be dumped. It is well known that the newer models have been reinforced with an outer casing that contains the nuclear mass for a critical fraction of a second until the atomic fire has time to kindle the whole explosive charge, thus completing the combustion and eliminating the 'smoke' that caused fallout and made the American bombs so cruel and ineffective. That is great progress on the part of Soviet scientists, and to my mind most humane."

"Humane indeed," the Deputy Premier agreed, not wishing to probe any deeper, thinking he now knew how to make a new bomb out of an old one, his mind working feverishly. In his mind he was framing a memo to his government. It would read, "When we get the bombs, reinforce them with an outer casing. Result will be conversion into pure energy, probably approaching 100 per cent of the well-known Einsteinian formula $E = mc^2$." He would astound his scientists with his knowledge. He would be made Premier.

"It has been a pleasure talking with you, Academician Anapolskoi," he said. "But these deep discussions are out of my field and I find myself a little fatigued. With your indulgence, I think I shall take a nap."

"Sleep well, my Transylvanian friend," Anapolskoi said, adding automatically an old Czarist benediction, "and Blessed Theotokos grant you holy dreams."

CHAPTER 3

In Panama, as Betty's time drew near, Bill Young set out to implement a pet project that had secretly occupied his mind ever since she had told him she was going to have a baby. He was proud of it, and it was to be a surprise. It was nothing less than a carefully thought out plan to take Betty away from the humid Base to the mountains of Jamaica, where she could wait for the baby in reasonable comfort and have it in what, for them, would be luxurious surroundings.

Of course he had a small air conditioner in the window in their bedroom, second-hand and half paid for, and it had made the summer Panama nights bearable. But there was no air conditioning in the stores where Betty shopped, and as a result she alternated between a sharp metallic-smellng night climate and the usual oppressive sticky air of the Panama Isthmus during daylight hours. She had never complained. Instead she had often remarked, "How wonderful it is to be so comfortable at night." But this was not enough for Bill, and so he schemed to get her out of Panama as soon in advance of the birth of the baby as he could get leave and his financial position would allow. It was part of his make-up to be quietly forehanded in the face of a challenge.

Panama, except for some crumble-prone, uninhabited mountains, is a flat and humid isthmus where malarial mosquitoes breed and, in the new state of the world since the advent of antibiotics, viruses of particularly unpleasant characteristics proliferate, viruses that cause colds and hang on for weeks and months, make you weak and groggy and upset your stomach, and cause even men to get sick like pregnant women, and then they invade the brain and bring on gloom and depression for no earthly reason, and the more sulpha the doctors fed you the weaker and gloomier you got. This was the firm conviction of petty officer Wilson Young. He was also certain that the Bermuda High caught up these viruses and swept them clockwise up north, and that was why everybody in the States always came down with a nagging summer cold nowadays. To get Betty away from the breeding ground of all this infection was one of the principal factors in his decision to take her to Jamaica; and now at last he could tell her about it.

"I got myself a thirty-day leave," he announced triumphantly one day. "We're going to have a real vacation, a real fancy vacation in Jamaica."

She had never been to Jamaica.

"In the mountains!" he added.

He stuck out his chest a little and grinned at the look of delight and bewilderment on her face. It had been a complete surprise.

"How in the world did you manage it?"

"Oh, the leave wasn't hard. There's nothing much doing."

"But the *money*, Bill."

"Oh, I'd saved a little."

"Bill, I know our bank account."

"Well, and I borrowed a little. You'd be surprised how good a petty officer's credit is."

"Oh Bill, you shouldn't have. You've never borrowed before."

"Well, I don't know a better time when a man ought to begin than when his wife's going to have a baby. Anyhow, I did it, and I'm glad. I've been planning this a long time."

Betty hugged him and her eyes looked dangerously close to tears.

"What's all this?" he said. "Aren't you glad? You look like you're going to cry."

"I'm crying because I *am* glad. Oh, Bill, I'm so happy!"

"Huh!" he said, planting a smacking kiss on each eye. "That's a woman for you. Cry when they're happy and cry when they're sad. Good thing I understand you."

No, she had not complained; but it had been very difficult for her in her heavy condition to go shopping and then cook their supper. The heat and the odors made her dizzy. She was always hungry but she had no taste for food after cooking it. As a result her face and her limbs continued to exhibit the photographer's fashion-model figure, but the rest, to her, looked grotesque.

"It's a good thing you're taking me someplace where people don't know me," she said. "My waist is up to forty inches."

"What was it before?"

"Oh Bill, it was twenty-four."

"Gosh," he said.

"I'm grotesque."

"To me," he said, "you are sweeter and lovelier than before."

She winced a bit at the "to me," as if he were admitting that everyone else must find her repulsive. Oh, they were respectful, exaggeratedly so, the Panamanian men who passed her on the street, but they either looked the other way or raised their big straw hats too ceremoniously; and of course the Americans just looked embarrassed.

"Well, I'd be mighty worried if you didn't look a little bigger. Suppose you were still twenty-four. Then I *would* be worried, and you would, too."

She laughed. "Yes, I guess I would. I'm thinking too much about myself. After all, it's all pretty normal, isn't it? I ought to be thinking about Wilson Young, Jr. He won't be an Englishman, will he, Bill, if he's born in Jamaica?"

"Good Lord, no. I looked into that. Children of American parents are American no matter where they're born. He wouldn't be an Eskimo if he was born at the North Pole, would he?" The thought tickled him. "Now that would be a real mix-up, wouldn't it? Eskimos are Mongolians. What a lot of angry fathers! No, Betty, he or she—we don't know it will be a boy, you know—will be just Bill or Betty Young."

"I was only joking, Bill. I was pretty sure he'd be a naturalized American."

"Not naturalized, honey. *Naturally*, just plain natural American, right from the minute he's born."

"Bill, I'm just a teeny bit scared. I wish it was over."

"There's nothing to it, nothing at all nowadays. They knock you out and you don't feel a thing."

"You certainly understand women," she said wryly. "*You* don't have to have them, you big lug." But she knew he was only trying to chase her nagging fears away and she'd have loved him less if he had done it less clumsily.

Bill went on to say that the town he had picked was a place called Las Palmas in an upland valley twenty miles from Kingston. Las Palmas stood at an elevation of four hundred feet and the cottage he had rented was on a mountainside six hundred feet higher, on a good road seven miles from the town, where there was a good modern hospital with a good staff of nurses and doctors. The house would be cool, and even taking into consideration the winding road, it wasn't more than fifteen minutes from the hospital. "I bet you can see it from the picture window; we've got a big picture window," he said. "It's down in the valley. We're on a hillside with a view of a great big beautiful green valley, and Las Palmas is right in the middle of it below us. Golly, the real estate in Jamaica!"

To be comfortable and at the same time to be so close to the hospital would give her confidence, he knew; and, for that matter, it would him too. He could get there fast if the baby decided to come at some ungodly hour, say, four o'clock in the morning, like he was always reading about in the papers. No taxi drivers, no police obstetricians for him, not for Wilson Young. He felt a glow of complacency. All in all he had done very well on a petty officer's pay. With a little foresight, which any ordinary father-to-be ought to exhibit at a time like this, he had provided his wife with the best possible surroundings in which to have his first-born. Anybody could do that. Why didn't everybody?

Generously, through channels, in no way unusual, the Navy gave Bill and Betty Young a free hike on a plane to Jamaica for Bill's thirty-day leave; and during that time another little American would see the light of day and, as averages went, would grow up to be very much like its parents, genes being what they are, in no way unusual, save perhaps that its life expectancy might be a few years longer than theirs, owing to advances in preventive medicine; and its education a little better, owing to America's perpetual preoccupation with social progress.

The plane was one of the last to leave Panama.

Later a curious thought struck Betty Young. Suppose the dove that old Noah released from the Ark, finding no rest for the sole of her foot, since the waters lay over the face of the whole earth, had returned to the place where the Ark had been—and the Ark had sunk, sunk beneath the waters, lost with every living thing aboard like the thousands of ships sunk in World War II.

For by the time Wilson Young, Jr. was born in Jamaica, something equally catastrophic and direfully analagous had occurred in the history of the planet.

CHAPTER 4

In Moscow, when the great delta-winged aircraft set down on the runway, Academician Anapolskoi made his report on his oceanographic studies in Panama; the cultural delegates made theirs on the World's Fair exhibit; and satellite Deputy Premier Karajan Chanuris made his to his Russian overlords, and it was political.

Chanuris' report made a good impression on the Kremlin officials. His attitude was correct and enthusiastic. True, he asked for atomic weapons for his government, as satellite officials always did. He said that his people would never feel themselves wholly integrated as equals in the Socialist world until the USSR equipped them with the means to defend themselves, and stated with some pride, which the Kremlin approved, that in defending themselves they would also be defending their good friends and preceptors, the giant USSR, to which they were bound in comradeship and to which they looked for guidance and inspiration. In Russian, in which it was couched, the verbiage shone with sincerity. Not a word had a diversional overtone. And the Kremlin was somewhat less rigid than it had been in the

32

early days of atomic secrecy. It felt confident, and it was weary of requests that it had to refuse: *all* the satellites were asking for bombs. After all, reasoned the Kremlin, the weapons were out of date. They recalled with a snicker that during World War II the Americans had actually classified information about a crossbow. Why not permit these Balkan patriots to play with some of the surplus? It could do no harm; it would soothe their egos; why not give these satellites a few obsolete bombs, and let them feel big and important and engage their loyalty, especially since with a minimum of alteration the bombs could be rendered far less destructive? Such a move, carefully edited and leaked to the world press, would serve as a counterweight against the Americans, who were known to have equipped their allies with nuclear weapons. In any event, the whole world would soon have them, since the simple principles of the early bombs were so well known that a competent schoolboy could construct one if given a modest machine shop and fissionable materials. Even Japan had just launched a rocket. A warhead would be next. There had never yet been a weapon that had been kept secret very long, from Greek fire through gunpowder to the atomic bomb.

In this realistic mood the Russian masters in the Kremlin gave Deputy Premier Karajan Chanuris what he wanted, fewer in quantity and lesser in yield; but he got them. He instantly went into a deep silence about what he had done with them, like a greedy child with a brand-new toy.

It is a mistake to underestimate the ingenuity of children. It is dangerous to put cutting toys into children's hands.

"Poor doddering old Jurassic Anapolskoi!" He laughed. "Even a Transylvanian knows what implosion is." He talked to his scientists about a reinforced outer casing, and rejoiced and felt his soul expand when they told him the principle was sound and the thing would probably work.

Deputy Premier Karajan Chanuris would gladly have laid down his life for his principles. Like a primitive Christian facing the beasts in the arena, he cared nothing for personal survival. A Cause burned within and consumed him. So long as The Cause was advanced, his own annihilation, which he deemed probable, was of no consequence. After victory a monument would be erected to him in Red Square, heart of the capital city of the ultimate Union of Soviet Socialist Republics of the World. The name Karajan Chanuris would be remembered forever by all future generations of school children, who would be taught how he had touched off the purge—he did not think of it as a war—which had cleansed the world of false ideologies and brought about the final destruction of Imperialist Capitalist Democracy.

Anapolskoi could have told him how a native of Sicily, a satellite state of no importance, had once had a similar dream for France. How was it that Napoleon was more French than the Frenchmen? And in his Jurassic heart Anapolskoi might have queried, "Or that Georgian, Stalin, more Russian than I?" And in his old-fashioned way he might have pondered the curiously apt analogy that the Devil himself was not originally a native of Hell.

At night Chanuris dreamed of his last burning moment, when his body would dissolve into its pure constituent elements in a fraction of a second in the very center of the fireball. During these dreams he longed passionately for that moment of extinction, the ultimate holocaust, so intense in its brilliance that the light, a light made one candlepower brighter by the burning of his body, could be seen from Mars; and, if there were men on Mars, they would note down the sudden illumination on earth in their history books. And one day they would know the truth: that Karajan Chanuris, single-handed, had wrought the sociological miracle that gave peace and brotherhood to Earth. In his mind the compulsion towards self-destruction was equated with love, since greater love hath no man than this, that he lay down his life for his friends. He identified himself with Jesus; he identified himself with God; he saw himself as the burnt offering on the altar. The images merged and glared and blinded him. Love mingled with worship and, in his dreams, which became waking dreams, he worshipped a new World Saviour, himself.

He saw the world through the twisted perspective of his own white-hot vision. This was the moment. This was the hour. This was for him, and the world was waiting for him, and he was there.

The Americans would not start the war, a war he hungered for, body and soul, as other men hungered for food or women or God: it was contrary to the Americans' decadent natures. He had studied their history. In their own revolution they had not fired first. Even the Russians seemed to be holding back. Perhaps they too were becoming soft, decadent, losing their ideals. But Deputy Premier Karajan Chanuris burned with the pure and primitive zeal. With Messianic integrity he felt called to show the Way.

If Chanuris had been a realistic man, like the pragmatists in the Kremlin, he would have foreseen the difficulties of starting a war single-handed. If he had been big and decent, like Anapolskoi, he would have shrunk, appalled, from the notion. If he had been an ordinary scoundrel, Russian Intelligence would quickly have arrested him and caused him to disappear. But there is no cunning, no daring, like the cunning and daring of the mad, and the most efficient intelligence organization never suspects them until it is too late.

Chanuris, who dreamed of liberating the world from the evil of imperialistic capitalism, hit upon the simplest of all stratagems, just as the fuse attached to a stick of dynamite is the simplest of all mechanisms.

Chanuris chose as the liberating mechanism a rusty old freighter, the *Jadwiga*, of Latvian registry. She was a perfect carrier for his cargo of wrath, since she was a patient old tramp, dependable, obscure and totally unsuspect. Her run for years had been from the Mediterranean to the west coast of South America and back, with general cargo each way. Her captain had been with her for years, and sometimes took his wife along for a cruise, a custom of older, better times. Her crew were devoted to their ship, and, though lazy and slow like the *Jadwiga,* would never have changed her for the sleeker, faster, more modern vessels.

Hidden among scores of identical packing boxes, marked "Cable" and consigned to a construction company in Valparaiso, Chile, was a vintage atom bomb. It was of the primitive Hiroshima type. Only the reinforced outer casing was new. Chanuris, working in secret, had conferred with his scientists and assured them that the thing was the most modern ever constructed. They had not dared to disagree, and indeed the implosion which he promised sounded so convincing that they were by no means sure the reconstructed bomb might not, as he said, transform itself into pure destructive energy at the moment of detonation.

At just the right time and in just the right place it would explode, and World War III would follow as a matter of course. He, the dedicated Deputy Premier of the patronized satellite nation, would start the cleansing war, since the cautious giants, now glowering at each other across their oceans, would not.

Chanuris chose the Pedro Miguel Locks of the Panama

Canal as the right place. The right time would be when the *Jadwiga* paused there, when the locks were closed, when the ship was immobilized by steel cables attached to six powerful mechanical "mules."

Lovingly, possessively, like a mother nursing the child she has created, a being that never existed before, Chanuris desired to be aboard the *Jadwiga* when it reached the Canal and personally assure the detonation of the bomb.

In his exultation he thought, I could *touch* the thing that will bring about the New Era. The world will date history from the event. Gone will be the old chronologies. All the old calendars will be out of date. They will name the New Era after me, not Anno Domini but *Anno Chanuri*, first a year, then another, then a hundred, then a thousand, then ten thousand, for my calendar will last forever. What a world, what a bright beautiful world there would be in A.C. 10,000!

Water was to be the bomb's triggering mechanism. A seacock would be opened in Number-Four Hatch, where the "Cable" packing boxes were, a simple turn of a valve. This would be done the minute the *Jadwiga* entered the Pedro Miguel Locks. Water would enter the bilge, rise in the hold and flood the hatch. It would engulf the packing boxes. There would be no telltale noise, no disorder; the boxes were heavy, they would not float; they would not bump against the bulkheads and betray the stratagem; they would rest there, and tier by tier in the darkness, pierced only by Chanuris' flashlight, for he would be there too, counting the seconds, they would disappear as the water level rose, so very, very silently.

Then, for Chanuris saw it all in his imagination, the *Jadwiga* would develop a list to starboard and settle at the stern, straining at the wire cables that tied her to the "mules," threatening to snap them since they were devised to maneuver a ship only on an even keel. It would cause consternation. Ships do not normally sink in the Panama Canal. They float upon the surface inert, their power off, obedient as logs on the way to the mill, while the "mules" inch them slowly ahead or hold them fast. A ship's captain need not even be on the bridge; he had delegated his command to the Canal Pilot, who signals the "mules" that inch the vessel through. A mood of relaxation envelops the crew, who have nothing to do but lean over the rail and shout greetings at similar crews on ships going in the opposite direction in the waterway alongside, for the Canal, like a divided highway with a mall in the center, is a two-way street with traffic in each direction. Often crews know each other, recognizing friendly ships, and they ask whether So-and-So is still madam of such-and-such an establishment in such-and-such a port, and what the current price of beer is, and some shout messages for sweethearts or even wives at home half round the world. But Karajan Chanuris would be in the hold, watching the water rise in Number-Four Hatch during this period of holiday relaxation.

When the list became apparent and the settling by the stern was noticed, there would be a commotion on the *Jadwiga's* deck, for such behavior in a vessel was unprecedented. The Letts and Lithuanians who made up her crew would rush about excitedly, shouting in languages which none of the American engineers alongside would understand. They would lean over the rail and point at the slowly rising waterline. The "mules" on the banks of the lock would stop; the steel lines would strain taut and snap; the American engineer in the control tower would phone frantically for emergency pumping equipment.

During that time the water would be rising in Number-

Four Hatch of the *Jadwiga,* pressing against the fuse of the bomb, building up the pressure that would detonate it. The fuse was a common device widely used in ordinary depth bombs. And there beside the thing, disguised as a wiper, the humblest of all jobs in the engine room, would be Deputy Premier Karajan Chanuris, waiting for the blast that he alone knew was seconds away.

In the voluminous inquiries which followed The Twenty Minute War it was established that something very like this must have actually occurred near the site of the Pedro Miguel Locks. Frogmen and deep-sea soundings placed an isolated area of persistent radioactivity in that vicinity and scientists speculate that that was the point of the original blast, though there were no survivors of the crew or dwellers in the former adjacent land areas to give direct testimony.

But Chanuris was not destined to disguise himself as a wiper, nor did he personally make the voyage in the *Jadwiga.*

Chanuris possessed that kind of madness which throughout history has attracted followers, and causes worry and self-reproach to the sane. One cannot contemplate a lunatic who hurls himself into martyrdom for his dreams without questioning one's own convictions, which are normally sober and balanced and, by contrast with the lunatic's, tepid. One thinks himself hesitant, cowardly. "Maybe the maniac is right," is the nagging self-reproach of the sane and slow in the moment of crisis. No such hesitation troubles the maniac.

Chanuris had on his staff a civil servant of peasant background named Karl Petkov, a man who had risen on merit and won his confidence through unquestioning fidelity and devotion: it was absolute; it was the hypnotic self-negation that soldiers had felt for Napoleon.

"Let *me* go!" Petkov begged. "I can run a tractor. I can

certainly open a seacock, which is much simpler. All you do is turn a valve, don't you, and the water comes in?"

"Yes," said Chanuris, hating him.

"You are needed here. I am expendable. Let me go." Chanuris glowered.

"You would be recognized, and the Russians would stop you," Petkov said, pleading.

The argument that a Deputy Premier was certain to be recognized weighed heavily with Chanuris. He was jealous of Petkov. Now Petkov, not Chanuris, would be the name remembered by immemorial generations of school children. Petkov, not Chanuris, would be worshipped as the new Salvator Mundi. The year 10,000 after the event would be A.P., not A.C. It was intolerable. But Chanuris knew he could not personally usher in the New Era of Peace.

Then a second thought prevailed. Was this not a greater immolation still? Like the Tetragrammaton, the secret name of God too sacred to speak, the name of Karajan Chanuris would never be spoken; but all the world would dwell in his presence and revere the great Unknown One who had wrought by stealth the miracle of the cleansing war.

So Chanuris sent Petkov in his stead, and Petkov it was who opened the seacock when the ship reached the Pedro Miguel Locks.

Having dispatched the *Jadwiga* the Deputy Premier became prey to an agonizing doubt. He had made one serious miscalculation; namely, blinded by the vision of eternal prominence, hungering for the perpetuity of his name, he had momentarily forgotten that he was a very well known political personage. It had taken the peasant Petkov to point out that he could neither disappear for a protracted period nor disguise himself among the crew of the *Jadwiga*, where he would be certain to be recognized.

Had he made any other miscalculations? His dreams became nightmares. In a spasm of self-accusation he heard himself confessing before the Soviet court, "I had the best of intentions, but I didn't bring it off. I expected instant war. You held back. So did the Americans. I did not believe them when they published their propaganda, 'One nuclear explosion will not trigger us into retaliation. It might be a mistake. It might be one of our own!'

"I thought this sort of pronouncement deliberately calculated to lull us to sleep. I thought they were trying to prove how tolerant and brave they were, when it has always been known that they are militantly aggressive. I thought they were trying to impress the world with how many bombs they had, when everyone knows we have more. I failed. I alone am guilty." On this the judges would agree, and he would take his place in the dismal procession of those who went to the wall, and with his mind's eye he followed the bullet that roared from the rifles of the firing squad and penetrated his breast and tore out his heart and splattered it against the wall and he died ignominiously. And still the New Era had not begun.

Suppose the Americans actually meant what they said and failed to press the button despite the explosion of the *Jadwiga?* The New Era would never come. Chanuris saw the Cold War stretching ahead for a thousand years, perhaps forever.

In Chanuris' mind no doubt ever lasted long, and the spectre of nonaction was unbearable.

He secretly dispatched another vessel, a nondescript river boat that habitually made trips up and down the Volga. She bore the old-fashioned name of *Ekaterina,* since the peasant crews of the Volga boats clung to the classic beloved names with little regard for more modern heroes. In the rotting

wooden bottom of the *Ekaterina* was another remodeled
bomb, designed to explode in the Russians' new Don-Volga
Canal, a magnificent piece of engineering the details of
which were jealously guarded and which very few Western-
ers were permitted to see.

"*That* will convince the sluggish Soviets it's time to press
the button," the Deputy Premier muttered. "It will look
like instant retaliation and drive the Kremlin mad." He
trembled with joy and hugged the scheme to his breast like
a lover. "Now we shall have action!"

As is now well known, we did.

The *Jadwiga* blew up, as far as can now be ascertained,
in the Pedro Miguel Locks. Regarding the uncertainty as to
the precise location of the first blast, it must be remembered
that there was a period of only an hour before the other
explosions supervened and that the reports were fragmentary and confused. Those who were telephoning and those
who were sending the more complicated coded messages by
cable and wireless were instantly consumed in The Twenty
Minute War. What has been salvaged, however, of their
early reports will never be entirely without interest.

One thing is certain. The super-weapon that Chanuris
imagined he had created simply did not work. He and his
scientists had erred. The reinforced casing accomplished
nothing but to make the fallout worse. The implosion,
though technically feasible if a casing could be made strong
enough to delay the blast, never occurred. He had failed to
provide a squeezing counterexplosion. Perhaps Anapolskoi
did not know this detail; perhaps he did not wish to explain
how it was done; or it may be that weaponry really bored
him, as he had stated on the plane. The *Jadwiga* blast was
thus of the primitive Hiroshima type and rather less in yield.

It was extremely dirty. The virulent fallout was caught up by the Bermuda High and carried over Mexico, on which it slowly sifted down, causing many ugly burns and much suffering among some individuals. But they are alive, and Mexico was spared the worst.

The Panama Canal was irretrievably blocked by the *Jadwiga* blast. The Pedro Miguel Locks were destroyed; water poured into Miraflores Lake and choked the spillway. It is not believed that the dam, which was very solid, collapsed at this point, though the head of radioactive water pouring over it must have reached a height of ten or twenty feet, and a number of ships progressing through the Lake were probably destroyed, hurtling over the dam like corks, unable to steam against the current.

This destruction of the Canal, though serious, had long been foreseen as a possibility by American military men. It meant a blocking of traffic between the Atlantic and Pacific Oceans, and temporary separation of the fleets in the event, deemed unlikely, that they would have to operate in concert. There were, however, detailed operational plans and quantities of equipment to redig the canal and rebuild the locks in such an emergency; and fleets of sea-, undersea- and aircraft had been long since deployed in accordance with a resourceful plan to minimize the blow. No enemy in his right mind would have failed to try to destroy the Panama Canal. No American Chief of Staff would have failed to foresee, discount and take measures against it.

News of the *Jadwiga* blast and the blocking of the Canal was instantly flashed to the White House by patrolling SAC planes, and the Kremlin knew of it almost as soon through their own Intelligence. Nothing else blew up, however, throughout the next hour, though on both sides long-prepared operations were set in motion to cope with the situation if it threatened to get out of hand. Missile pilots clambered into their detachable capsules and scanned their charts, pinpointing their destined landing areas in friendly countries after they had let their lethal loads down on enemy targets. The automatic rockets were armed and their guidance systems set. All over the world the older craft were alerted and their crews stood to the ready. But during the first hour no order to strike went out from the White House or from the Kremlin. Both sides, while they cocked their nuclear guns, held their fire. It might have been a tragic mistake. No one wanted to blunder into war.

It is known that during the first two minutes of that quiet hour the White House telephoned the Kremlin and the Kremlin telephoned the White House. It may lighten this somber narrative to report a most ludicrous fact, now incontestably authenticated . . . the operators actually reported that the line was busy. It could hardly have been otherwise, since the President and the Russian Premier were calling each other simultaneously. Socrates said, "The genius of Tragedy and Comedy is essentially the same." Shortly the error was rectified, the private channel of communication was cleared and the two men found themselves speaking to each other.

The importance of this slight delay in establishing personal contact between the heads of state has been much dramatized and exaggerated. The deterrent effect of the phone call would have been nil even if it had started sooner and been carried to completion. Karajan Chanuris had seen to that with diabolical cleverness in planting the *Ekaterina* bomb.

There is no tape of the conversation, as was inevitable in view of what followed; but monitors in Scotland and Hawaii, who heard them, have testified that both men talked at the same time, shouting over their interpreters, protesting their good intentions, agreeing that the Panama explosion might be some horrible accident, yelling at each other to keep calm.

Then it was that the *Ekaterina* exploded in the Don-Volga Canal. The Russians leaped to the conclusion that while the telephone conversation was actually in progress, the Americans, stalling for time, had struck by some secret, insidious, long-prepared device. This drove them mad, as Chanuris had planned.

Then it was that the buttons were pushed on both sides, and the missiles, both manned and automatic, roared into the sky.

Thus started the war which, by reason of its extraordinary shortness, came to be called The Twenty Minute War.

By an odd coincidence the historian Toynbee, a gloomy Englishman, had foreseen its duration with formidable exactitude. Studying the length of wars from the fifteenth to the twentieth centuries, he had charted how long they lasted and, projecting his curves into the future, had reached the conclusion that the next world war would be virtually instantaneous.

Virtually, his charts came true.

The history of The Twenty Minute War may be likened to a duel between two men who meet on a field and kill each other with a single shot from each pistol.

On radar screens, that volatilized within minutes, the blips of approaching rockets were observed. On spidery radio telescopes, that shortly melted, they were heard as a series of rising musical notes, interspersed with ominous but unintelligible hissing sounds. On sonar devices the Russian submarines were heard to surface, and no one doubted that they were launching their missiles from positions close off the shores of the entire American continent. On the world-wide web of watching stations, kept secret from their own people but well known to the enemy, both sides saw the rockets rise in volleys. Then the mechanical eyes of the watching stations were atomized, for all were geographically pinpointed and all were blinded according to plan. Here and there one would escape total destruction and continue to broadcast its frantic warning upon a void, for by that time the world did not need to be warned. The personnel of the missed stations, however, died as surely as those who were hit, but less quickly.

Not all of the war was rocketry. The war effort was total. On both sides the older weapons were used. SAC planes roared into the air, but by the time they reached their targets they dropped their bombs on cities already reduced to craters by the rockets. Similarly futile were three hundred Russian armored divisions, which revved up their tanks and troop transports for a dash to the west, only to discover boundaries nonexistent and their objectives already obliterated by more modern means. These old-fashioned maneuvers were later much smiled at, and equated with the retention of crossbows and catapults by armies of the fifteenth century long after gunpowder had been invented, but since no one could foresee the power of the perfected nuclear explosions it was deemed a wise precaution at the time, like sails on the first steamboats and bayonets on rifles.

Here it will be well to devote a moment to Deputy Premier Karajan Chanuris and how he met his end, lest his wicked name be forgotten.

In his chancellery he suffered an agony of uncertainty awaiting reports of Petkov's exploit in the Panama Canal. When news came that the *Jadwiga* had successfully exploded he was dissatisfied with the results. He had hoped for something more spectacular. He blamed Academician Ana-polskoi for telling him a lie. The bomb did not achieve $E = mc^2$. He bit his nails till they bled waiting for the *Ekaterina* explosion. That came too, and he laughed for joy.

Still, there was an hour's wait, and during that time he ex-perienced a deep fit of depression.

Then came the news that both sides had finally launched their most lethal missiles in a saturation barrage; and for a time Karajan Chanuris was the only happy man in the world. The Cleansing War had finally begun! The great ideologies were locked in mortal combat. The wicked capi-talist imperialist nations would be obliterated. Socialism would win. The Cause had conquered. And to Karajan Chan-uris, with no monument in Red Square, with no mention in the history books, would rightfully belong the credit, yes, even the worship of all ages to come for the inestimable benefits he had wrought. He was content.

And then came an ominous silence, and The Pause. He railed at his aides for information, but there was none. Slowly, bit by bit, item by item, fragmentary reports began to filter in. He began to fit them together, like pieces of a jigsaw puzzle. They formed a picture so different from anything he had expected, so horribly destructive of his ideal, that at first he contemplated suicide. Even that was denied him. His delicately balanced mind gave way altogether. Karajan Chan-uris went mad and ceased to be a menace to himself, far less to the world he had so grievously harmed. Those who brushed by him in his office, before he was swept into dis-card like a broken crock, say he gave the appearance of a harmless lunatic. He had never been a robust man. Now he seemed to have shrunk physically in stature. His hair turned white and he whimpered and drooled one sentence, one only: "My work is done and I am dead and I am immortal." He was deemed unfit even to handle a pick and shovel. How he actually died in the welter of death that now spread round the planet has never been inquired.

What drove Chanuris mad, as it did many men, was that the missiles had found their targets, found them on both sides of the separating oceans, with a dire and unexpected effect that far outstripped the most sanguine hopes of the military men who pressed the buttons.

There was no formal end to The Twenty Minute War. No diplomats sat around green felt-covered tables or haggled over peace terms or jockeyed for positions of advantage. In the twinkling of an eye the diplomats, the leaders and presidents, premiers and dictators on both sides died in the multiple and accurately aimed explosions, and new leaders arose in their stead. It was not necessary to stop The Twenty Minute War. It stopped itself. No one had time to haggle over peace terms. Peace came as a matter of course, as it does to fighting animals upon whom stalks a stronger enemy.

There was now work to do, a work so big as to be almost impossible of accomplishment. But if it were not accomplished Death waited and grinned over the entire planet. It was not a gruesome death since freezing is not painful, but it was Death all the same. There the Monster stood, astraddle the poles, advancing, inexorable, older than the wheel, older than the taming of fire, ice cold and prehistoric.

CHAPTER 5

In continental Russia, where the American missiles had fallen upon the principal cities including Moscow with its nerve centers of communications, those cities disappeared. The same held true for Washington and America's productive industrial areas. Britain and Western Europe also suffered heavily, as did the Soviet satellites. Figures compiled after the war in the voluminous studies that were made, admitting a probable margin of error of 20 per cent, placed the world dead at two hundred million.

Still, this was not the end of the world. It was less than 10 per cent of the planet's total population. There had been plagues in the Middle Ages that swept away 25 per cent of the population. There had been wars more deadly, proportionately, in former ages, notably The Thirty Years War, that killed 30 per cent. In a single generation Nature had always been able to make up the loss. Decimation was not annihilation.

It was not, therefore, the reparable diminution of mere numbers of the human race that brought an end to The Twenty Minute War but the unexpected occurrence in Pan-

ama, an occurrence that fitted squarely into the specialized
study of Academician Anapolskoi and for which his help was
required.

Anapolskoi survived the war. From Panama he had gone
to the Arab side of the Jordan to make deep soundings of
the Dead Sea. The Russian scientists had speculated that the
hydrogen sulphide that bubbled up from the Dead Sea bottom might be tapped in caissons and processed for commercial use in the manufacture of hydrochloric acid, a chemical
required for industrial fertilizers and traditional explosives.
Now Academician Anapolskoi's specialized knowledge was
needed to explain the disaster in Central America and propose remedial measures.

Panama, where the trouble had started and where it was
feared that massive retaliatory installations might still exist,
was a prime target and drew more than its share of missiles,
with disastrous results to both sides. All homed unerringly
in on target, the automatic rockets with the wonderful di-
recting devices that had hit the moon like a bull's-eye and
the manned missiles whose pilots detached their capsules
after aiming the body of their rockets and sailed on to sanctuary in friendly states. Equally accurate were the American
missiles. It has been remembered with irony that the élite
corps of missile pilots were the safest men in the world during the short period of actual hostilities, far above the holocaust below.

It was at first taken as a good omen that these new nuclear
weapons, wherever they exploded, were remarkably "clean,"
that is to say, free of radioactive fallout. Their cleanliness
was due to their vastly improved efficiency, their approach
to conversion of mass into energy closer than anything ever
before accomplished by man.

Indeed, the conversion was too close; the results were unanticipated. Then it was remembered with trepidation that something very similar had happened when the first hydrogen bomb went wild and mystified its creators. It was exploded on an island in the Pacific. That island had "burned" for two hours, till in the end it was totally consumed. Nothing was left but a hole in the ocean floor. The nature of the burning was not understood.

In the Isthmus of Panama the same thing, magnified millions of times, had occurred the moment the awesomely accurate and hideously improved Soviet bombs began to fall. From Montería in Colombia to Leon in Nicaragua the whole slender thread of Central America, a distance of seven hundred miles, began to burn with unquenchable atomic fire. It lighted the summer sky all over the night side of the globe with a weird white light which was brighter than the sun and the color of which was remembered with horror, for it had none of the sunlight's pleasant yellow warmth, which is associated in human hearts with springtime, flowers and the awakening of life, but rather the glare of an oxyhydrogen torch, which is designed to sever and slice. The inexplicable burning of the Isthmus lasted ten hours, well into the next day. And when it was night again, the Central American republics of Costa Rica and Panama, together with significant portions of Nicaragua and Colombia, were gone. Over the area which the Isthmus had occupied there was boiling water. This was the wild phenomenon that Academician Anapolskoi was called upon to explain to the Supreme Soviet, which was most depleted, newly elected and very frightened. Virtually all the old members were dead.

"It is not scientifically accurate," Academician Anapolskoi said, "to state that all these countries 'sank beneath the waves,' though the sea rolls forty fathoms deep in the area lately occupied by the isthmian lands and the common run of folk use the term 'sunk' or 'submerged.' In actuality, the material substance of this seven-hundred-mile stretch of land was atomized and thrown up into the stratosphere. I do not conceive that the so-called burning which was observed could have represented the conversion of matter into pure energy, since a transmutation of such magnitude would have blown the planet to bits. Rather it must be supposed that the matter of the Isthmus was pulverized and hurled into the upper atmosphere in the form of colloidal dust. The appearance of the sunrise and sunset as now experienced, and the dark days, are reminiscent of conditions after the volcanic explosion of the island of Krakatoa and would seem to bear out this hypothesis."

And indeed the days were dark all over the world as if a high but persistent cloud hovered over it at a great distance. The stuff of the cloud, however, was so fine that even when it sifted down, sometimes in a red rain, sometimes in a curiously rosy fog, there was no difficulty in breathing. Nor was there any perceptible rise in radioactivity in samples taken from the air.

"Fallout was limited on the American side to some sporadic instances in Mexico, which were due to the *Jadwiga* bomb, and to the Don-Volga area where another old-fashioned bomb exploded. There has been some speculation, of course, that the white light that we all observed while the perfected new missiles were falling may have been harmful, since the loosing of such vast amounts of energy is something new in science. Some have speculated that this light was like the cosmic rays, which the earth's atmosphere largely screens out, and have been worried because these were generated within the earth's atmosphere, indeed at the very bottom of the ocean of air that surrounds us all and where we all live. But I deem it likely that whatever damage was done to living organisms, if any, must have been genetic, occurring in the first millisecond and propagated in waves traveling at the speed of light, dissipating itself largely into space and striking very few."

Academician Anapolskoi's optimistic genetic report was given in the early days of The Pause, when both sides were assessing their losses, choosing new leaders, the old leaders being all dead, and preparing for the second round of the war.

The second round never came, although at the time both sides, like wounded beasts, would probably have fought to the death had not Death already hovered close.

The total annihilation of seven hundred miles of Central America wrought an oceanic change that reduced The Twenty Minute War to absurdity, and it simply stopped. In this stoppage the spectacular sunsets also played a part.

Inasmuch as it will shortly be required of the reader to follow the work of Academician Anapolskoi in some detail, particularly as regards the Gulf Stream, which is warm, and the Humboldt Current, which is cold, lying in their separate oceans, it would be well at this point to record one happy event in this somber narrative.

Wilson Young, Jr. was born in the hospital at Las Palmas in Jamaica without pain to his mother, she being deep in twilight sleep, and to his father's immense and thoroughly normal joy. The birth was without complication and Betty was soon up and around again.

The birth came at midnight and the only abnormal circumstances attendant upon it were the noises underground, which the mother could not hear through the haze of drugs, and the light in the sky; and as for the child, so recently emerged from the dark of her womb, he as yet had no experience and as yet had learned nothing and seemed quite content to breathe the air of a world he had not made, like billions of babies before him. He took his first breath with a healthy cry before they cut the cord.

He appeared in every respect quite average, like his parents, exactly as they had hoped he would be, subject always, of course, to the natural ambition which parents have that their youngsters will advance a step beyond their own station in life, yet not so far that they lose contact.

Then suddenly, in August, in the gaping hole that had been London, and all the other holes that had been all the great cities of the northern latitudes, the temperature dropped and it began to snow.

The snow continued.

PART TWO

THE BIG ICE

CHAPTER 1

WHEN Betty Young awoke next day, remembering little of
the birth because of the twilight sleep that had eased the
entry of Wilson Young, Jr. into the world, she asked to see
the baby. A nurse brought him to her.

Betty noticed that the nurse wore a white surgical mask
and, reaching up to her own face, discovered that she wore
one too. She smiled beneath the gauze and gave the Las
Palmas Hospital a good mark for sanitation.

But it was peculiar that the baby also wore one.

"What is it, nurse?" she asked. "A boy or a girl?"

It was a dear little thing with brown eyes, very big and
bright. She had heard that newborn babies' eyes were always
blue, with blue even suffusing the whites, and that later
they took on their permanent color. These eyes were the
eyes of a much older child, with the whites pure white and
the brown clearly defined. For a moment Betty felt a twinge
of panic and wondered whether there had not been a mistake in the nursery. She had read of inexplicable mix-ups
despite footprints and all the other modern precautions.

"A boy, Mrs. Young," said the nurse, and tucked him into the crook of Betty's arm.

Betty reached over and pulled down the child's mask. "I want to see his face," she said.

The nurse immediately replaced the infant's mask. Betty looked up in bewilderment.

"Orders," the nurse said, and hurried out.

Betty shrugged. In the instant while her baby's face was exposed she had got a glimpse of its smooth and handsome little countenance, not at all like the red, wrinkled skin of some babies, and the mouth seemed to be smiling at her. She saw in it her husband's face mysteriously and beautifully merged with her own. There had been no mix-up. The baby was hers and Bill's, and her heart melted and she loved it exceedingly.

"You darling!" she whispered, and hugged him close.

The child looked up at her quizzically, seemed to understand, gurgled and sought her breast in a determined fashion. Betty smiled, gently bared his face again and he nursed. Shortly he went to sleep, nestling his head against her breast, breathing deeply and contentedly, snoring a baby snore.

Betty hesitated to replace the surgical mask for fear it would interfere with his breathing, since she did not know whether babies usually snored or not. It sounded like Bill, that snoring, and it was very cute. She would say to her husband, "Bill, Billy snores, just like you!" But it might be phlegm in his nasal passages and she did not want to make it hard for him to breathe the first air he had ever breathed. How foolishly strict the Las Palmas Hospital must be to mask a newborn child as well as the mother. What nonsense.

So, for some moments, she looked at him and felt his warm cheek against her body and said to him, "Billy boy, you still feel like part of me, as yesterday you were. Now we are two instead of one. I almost want to surround you again and keep you where you were, even if you did make me sick a lot longer than most babies." The child slept on and Betty reproached herself, "No, that was possessive." From now on the mite in the crook of her arm would make his own way in the world, growing ever farther away from the womb that had sheltered and borne him, till he grew up to be a crewcut youth, then a man like his father, more distant every year till, perhaps, he became an admiral with stern sea wrinkles around that hungry little baby mouth and a roar of command in the throat that as yet could only gurgle and search towards her breasts.

"Darling," she whispered and hugged him tighter. It was a glorious moment. She wondered where Wilson Young, Sr. was, and smiled. The child, by its mere existence, had added a title to the father, "Senior," as if Bill Young were an old man instead of a young petty officer at the very beginning of his naval career.

Where *was* her husband?

Wasn't it protocol for the husband to follow in the wake of the nurse, beaming and bumptious and proud of his achievement, especially when it was a boy?

She was drifting off into sleep again and before she did she wished Bill would come in and view their new son. No doubt he had already seen him while she was still drowsy from the drugs, but it would be nice for him to come in now for a first appraisal of the Wilson Young family, all three in one room.

A doctor with a harried look in his eyes—that was all of his face she could see, since the doctor too wore a mask—suddenly entered, reached down and pulled the gauze up over the baby's nose.

"This must be kept on," he said abruptly.

"Why?"

"Orders," said the doctor severely.

"Where is my husband?"

"Please do not worry," the doctor said. "Just be sure to keep the mask on, except when you nurse him. Do try to keep the feeding times short."

Betty bristled. "Where is Bill? Why isn't my husband here?"

"Put her to sleep," the doctor said in a low voice. "She doesn't know what has happened." Then he hurried out.

Perhaps my sense of time is askew, Betty thought. She had never been through this before and was not quite sure what to expect. But everyone in Las Palmas certainly did seem to be terribly preoccupied and moving very fast.

She felt the needle in her arm and as she slipped into unconsciousness she felt the nurse remove the baby from her side.

"Everything is all right," said the nurse in a voice that seemed to come from a great distance. "I'll tell you all about it when you wake up."

The hypo was strong. This was no time for ordinary measures. In the emergency everything was exaggerated. Dosages were doubled, people spoke curtly, short cuts were taken and no words wasted.

Yes, it was certainly a strictly run hospital, Betty thought, and shortly lapsed into an uncomfortable dream, where the weather was abominably hot. She dreamed that she was Lilith, a pre-Adamite demon who lived in the world all alone, female and predatory, and, after Adam was created, became his first wife. But Lilith proved unworthy and the Good Lord dismissed her and substituted Mother Eve, who

proved better, if only by a little. In her dream she remembered an old poem about Lilith. She was . . .

> Born when Creation shook,
> Nurtured with thunderbolts,
> Tutored by demons and
> Wooed in a tempest . . .

Betty fought at the dream, clinging to her identity. She was
not the demon Lilith, and her instructors at the University of
Wisconsin had not been demons, and it was very unfair of
the dream to frighten her; but it continued . . .

> Gravid with monsters that
> Clawed in her belly;
> Labored eternities,
> Wept as she spawned them.

She had seen the child, and he was no monster; and if she
had wept a bit when he was born, she did not remember.
There was more to the horrid poem in the uncomfortable
dream:

> Flooded the sounding hot
> Ocean of Chaos up,
> Challenging order decreed by the Lord . . .

It sounded like something pre-Genesis, folklore enshrined
in the writing of some idiotic poet, whose name she could
not remember and she did not wish to. But even in her
dream she could not shake the conviction that the weather
was very hot and the notion of a seething flood encircling
her seemed very real. She knew she was dreaming; she
wished she would wake up. But two lines remained . . .

> Yet from her tears sprang
> Brave the New World.

When she awoke, Bill was at her bedside wiping her eyes, muttering soothingly, "It's all right, honey; it's all right."

She sat bolt upright in the bed. On the tip of her tongue was an accusation, "Bill, did you woo me in a tempest?" but as her mind cleared she recognized the absurdity of the words. Anyhow, it was in a canoe in Lake Mendota.

"I had an awful dream," was all she said.

She could still feel the heat, however; that was no dream; and there was a dense fog outside the hospital windows. From time to time big drops of red dusty rain would splatter against the panes. Bill was in battle dress and he held the baby in his arms.

The child was still masked but its intelligent eyes looked at her as if he remembered her. Bill put him in her arms and the infant reached out his little hands and sought her breast and nursed.

"Hey, you're a smart one!" Bill said, laughing.

But Betty knew it was only lucky fumbling on the part of a child not yet a day old.

"I only have a minute," Bill said more gravely. There were worry wrinkles on his tanned forehead.

She said, "What is the matter? Why is everyone wearing those silly gauze things? Is something wrong with the baby?"

He shook his head. "Not a thing."

"Why did they give me that hypo? It knocked me out like a light. I felt fine. I still do."

He briefed her.

During the night he had paced the floor outside the delivery room, asking the usual questions and getting the usual answers from nurses, who seemed to have learned the art of saying nothing in nursing school. No, it was not yet time. No, it was not an abnormally long delivery. Yes, everything was going fine. Yes, the doctor was still with her.

And, till the white light glared, there was the usual bantering hospital humor, "We've never lost a father yet."

Then the weird illumination had appeared on the western horizon, and no one smiled after that.

The phenomenon appeared at first as a pinpoint of fire, as if some unfortunate ship were in distress. Then it blossomed into a low semicircle of glow, like a full moon rising, if the moon could rise in the west. Then it grew in intensity and filled the whole horizon, reaching the zenith.

At the beginning there was no sound. Whatever it was, therefore, it must be far away and pose no threat to Jamaica, but it was frightening.

Jamaica possesses one of the best weather bureaus in the Western Hemisphere, lying as it does dead center in the spawning ground of the tropical storms that from time to time sweep up and devastate the east coast of the United States. The Kingston *Times* immediately called the weather bureau about the glow. The weather bureau had no quick answer, for within minutes military censorship clamped down a security blackout. All the *Times* got was a mumbled speculation about sunspots and ionization before the weatherman's voice became indistinct.

The *Times* then queried the U.S. Naval Base at Portland Bight and received the answer, "Contact London."

There was, of course, no longer a London.

Exactly one minute and twenty-five seconds later these conversations were interrupted by a thump like an earthquake that smote the roots of the island from under water. It was not an earthquake; no buildings fell; it was a massive abdominal growl from the bowels of the earth. It was traveling at the rate of one mile every five seconds throughout the length and breadth of the Caribbean Sea. It smashed into the seacoasts of Texas and Florida. It buffeted against Venezuela and reached out across the Atlantic towards Europe, killing fish and warping the steel plates of ships, springing leaks. It reached the island of Jamaica and caused it to vibrate like a sounding board, and the vibrations became audible to human ears as they were transmitted to the air. It sounded like a deep sustained animal growling, and it seemed to come from everywhere: from earth, from sea, from sky. And all the while the white light glared.

Exactly two minutes after the first appearance of the light another wave of sound, this time propagated through the atmosphere, burst upon the island. This noise was sharper; the monster barked, like a succession of artillery detonations, then rose in pitch till it shrieked like a million giants screaming, acompanied by a continuous rumble like distant thunder.

It was the death rattle of Central America, burning, as the super missiles, with their hideously improved clean fission war heads, fell upon it, consuming it.

Lost in the mightier holocaust was the devastation of the *Jadwiga* blast; lost was the first baby cry of Wilson Young, Jr., who, at that moment, was leaving the protecting flesh of Betty's womb, naked in a world those older and wiser had made for him; and, like all children, he would play his part in remaking it. Other babies were being born at the precise moment he saw the light, too bright a light, and were subject to the same influences that were to shape his body and mind.

Little by little, piece by piece, the enormity of the catastrophe seeped into Betty's groggy, reluctant brain.

"But it's war, Bill!" she cried.

"It sure is," he said.

"You'll have to go away from me now."

"I'm afraid so. But I haven't any orders yet. Just stand-by orders."

"We must go home."

By "home" he knew she meant the Base in Panama.

"It's destroyed, Betty. There's nothing left there. Not even the land. It's gone. The whole place, land and all, it just disappeared. I don't see how it could happen, but they say all Panama burned up."

"All the houses, all the people, all the women and babies? Oh *Bill!*"

"It's a lot worse than that. The whole damned country disappeared. Maybe the force of the blasts pushed it under water. Anyhow, SAC planes have reconnoitered the whole area looking for it. Ships and subs can't get near yet. It's still too hot. But the pilots say Panama isn't there any more, and they've photographed everything and the pictures come out blank. They tried infrared film—that'll usually get through fog, only this is steam—and they've tried radar. There's just nothing but water, and it's mighty hot."

It was incredible. It was a physical impossibility. She could understand rubble and blown-up cities. She had read about Hiroshima and Nagasaki. But her mind could not grasp the annihilation of Panama, and Bill said it might be all of Central America.

Fatuously, she said, "Are you sure?"

She knew the answer in advance. Bill was a practical man, not given to flights of fancy.

"Sure I'm sure," he said.

"What will we do, Bill?"

He grinned and nodded his head towards the red-stained window. "We just sit tight, I guess, and try to keep cool till I get my orders from Omaha."

"Omaha?"

Washington, he told her, was a deep, round hole in the ground, rapidly filling with water from Chesapeake Bay; London was another lake, filling with Thames water. As for Moscow—well, he smiled crookedly, we wouldn't have to worry about Moscow. It was gone too, and all the industrial cities of Russia. "Our missiles were right on target," he said.

He took out his handkerchief and wiped the beads of perspiration from her brow, then wiped his own with the back of his hand. "I tried to have an air conditioner brought in here," he said, "but I couldn't convince them that you were a critical patient. All the air conditioners are reserved for the operating rooms and for critical patients. The temperature is 106° outside."

"Why is it so hot, Bill?"

It was the missiles, he said. They had heated the air when they exploded. It would soon blow over. The sea water too was hot. Reconnaissance planes reported that over the area where Panama had been the ocean was still boiling. Boiled fish and cooked lobsters had been washed ashore. Many poor people had eaten them till teams of defense workers with Geiger Counters rushed in and warned that they might be contaminated. But the Geiger Counters registered no rise in radioactivity, and the poor people were left with their pitiful bonus of manna from The Twenty Minute War and ate it in safety and thanksgiving.

Betty sensed that Bill was anxious to get aboard his ship and fight back at the instigators of the cruel attack; but selfishly she was glad that so far his orders kept him in Jamaica near her and the boy. Soon enough he would get new orders —from Omaha!—to go off somewhere and fight. Meanwhile she had him.

"Where will they send you, Bill?"

"I don't know. Wherever we can do any good."

"I hope they keep you here."

He patted her shoulder and looked at Bill Young, Jr. "Not likely," he said.

"Bill, was everybody in Washington killed?"

"I guess so. That's what they say."

"Everybody in the Pentagon, everybody in the White House? The President? The whole government?"

"That's what they say."

"But you've got to have a President. Who's the new President?"

Bill suddenly realized that he had no idea. He remembered vaguely that the presidential succession starts with the Vice President and runs down through the members of the Cabinet and, after nine or ten removes, lands somewhere in the Senate or House of Representatives.

"Everything's sort of mixed up right now, Betty, but we must have some kind of Commander-in-Chief. We're still getting orders. From Omaha. Probably there was some arrangement for a government to function from there if something like this happened. There's got to be somebody in authority no matter what happens."

CHAPTER 2

In Russia too there was provision for authority in case of disaster. Academician Anapolskoi was summoned and flown by jet from the Dead Sea, where his H_2S experiments were now useless, to the Metal Workers Palace in Magnitogorsk behind the protecting shield of the Ural Mountains. There as yet no bombs had fallen. He was one of a distinguished group of scientists called upon to give his opinion before the decimated and hastily convened Supreme Soviet on the best means for further vigorous prosecution of the war.

To Academician Anapolskoi the world owes The Pause and the fact that Round Two of The Twenty Minute War never took place, though he was actuated by no humanitarian motives at this critical juncture. He was a patriotic Russian; now that war had come, he wanted Russia to win. His hearers were equally patriotic, but their confidence was shaken and they were in a retaliatory mood. He knew they wanted rousing words and scientific optimism. He did the best he could.

But facts were facts.

Anapolskoi said: "First, if my comrades will indulge me, let me make clear, if my white hair does not already stress

68

the fact, that I am somewhat elderly and that, though I share
the zeal of my younger comrades for victory, my specialized
field of study lies in a different area from theirs and I must
respectfully decline to advise whether we can or cannot
carry this war to its desired conclusion, namely, that Holy
Mother Russia emerge triumphant, and I pray she may."

(It was here, when Anapolskoi used the old-fashioned
term "Holy Mother Russia" that some members, particularly
from the hot-headed satellite republics, left the chamber.)

He continued: "But my discipline is one in which I observe how one species of organism survives attack and sup-
plants organisms with which it is in conflict. I cite in evidence the emergence of Man, supplanting the dinosaurs. But
did the mammal Man triumph because he actually slew those
reptiles? The time scale is against this explanation. Or did
the reptiles succumb and mammal Man arise because of a
climatic change? I deem the latter hypothesis more likely."

(Here some members yawned, but the emergency was
acute and everyone must be heard.)

"Now we are engaged in a great ideological war, to deter-
mine whether the world can live half-capitalist and half-
Marxian–socialist. The physical fact of the existence of the
war raises grave doubt in my mind that it can; but I am not
qualified to discuss sociological subtleties, which I willingly
leave to my colleagues who make sociology their study.

"But one element of this war, in its present state, presents
an aspect which falls within the purview of my own discipline, indeed it may be said to lie at its core. On this I have
been asked to comment."

("What a tedious opening! How long will he speak?" asked
the Deputy from Georgia. "Be still, and listen!" whispered the
Deputy from Outer Mongolia, who had later news.)

Anapolskoi continued: "As is well known, our missiles

have destroyed a seven-hundred-mile stretch of the Isthmus of Panama."

(Loud cheering.)

When the chamber quieted down, he remarked, "I join the acclamations of my comrades if indeed this event is to our advantage."

(Shouts of "Advantage! Advantage! Yes!")

"But the obliteration of the Isthmus of Panama may be something to give us pause."

From this chance phrase of a British poet "The Pause" took its name.

"It may well be," said the old academician in a somber voice, "that we have destroyed something we cannot replace. Central America, from its watery grave, may turn upon us and exact a fearful vengeance. Unless my charts err, and I have some pride in them, we have seriously upset the flow of the Gulf Stream. A slow death by freezing quite possibly awaits every deputy in this room. Nay, more, every man, woman and child now alive on the face of the earth, friend and foe alike, may face the universal threat of extinction. I do not say it will happen. More study is required. But I say it is possible."

While Academician Anapolskoi was speaking, queer things were happening in remote parts of the northern hemisphere.

CHAPTER 3

On the Russian steppe near Sherkaly, close to the Arctic Circle, a Tartar herdsman named Luka rubbed his eyes and squinted up at the sky in disbelief. This was the time of year when his reindeer fattened on the luxuriant vegetation that flourished under the bright sunshine of the eighteen-hour-long day.

But today the sun was not clear. It looked copper-colored and angry as if it were trying to fight its way through a very high fog. There was an autumnal chill in the air. "Six weeks early," he muttered. The herd was restless.

Luka trudged home to consult with his wife. Like all older-generation Cossacks he never made a decision without her. By now she would probably have listened to the news in the Sherkaly market place where a big loud speaker was set up on a pole. Every day at noon there was a newscast and a weather report. In summer the forecast was always the same: fair, clear, warm, little change in temperature; no precipitation. But today Luka suspected there was something wrong with the weather, and if so, the radio would have explained it.

His wife was waiting at the door of the house, which was spacious and well furnished according to Cossack standards. She leaned on her broom, which was made of the same stiff steppe grass as the thatch of the roof.

"Lukashka," she called to him, addressing him by the affectionate diminutive of his name, "there is war again. They broadcast the news in Cossack and *Russian*."

"Hé, little old mother," Luka said, "then it is a very big war. When we fought the wicked Fascist Nazis the radio spoke to us only in Cossack." It was consistent Soviet policy to encourage the seventy languages and dialects of its people. Only in cases of extreme urgency were the broadcasts repeated in Russian.

"What did the radio say about the weather, old mother?"

"There was no weather report, Lukashka."

"There is always a weather report."

"This day there was none."

"Moscow should keep us better informed," he said suspiciously.

"The broadcast did not come from Moscow," his wife said. "All official broadcasts will come from Magnitogorsk from now on."

"You are old and hard of hearing," the herdsman said. "Go back tomorrow and listen more carefully."

"Moscow is a hole in the ground."

"And you're drunk," Luka said, not unkindly, since it was chilly and she deserved a nip. Her flat Tartar face would have appeared impassive to a Westerner, but to Luka's Tartar eyes it was tight with worry and full of emergency.

"Listen tomorrow more carefully," he said; and she saw in his emotionless expression the reflection of her own fears.

That night the sun set red and threatening. During the

night the temperature, already chill, plummeted downward and, incredibly, snowflakes that looked as if they were tinged with blood filtered down. The reindeer whimpered and huddled together.

CHAPTER 4

On the motor road between Kalgan, on the frontier of China, and Ulan Bator, capital of the Mongol Peoples Republic, Ahmed Timur, the trader, honked the horn of the leading truck and signaled the hour of prayer. It was sunset. Islam set aside this time to praise Allah, and after that it was time for the caravan to take to the road again following the day's halt in the torrid heat. The young Chinese laborers, who were strapping Communist atheists, stood by expressionless while Timur and his Moslem drivers knelt in the dust beside the trucks, facing Mecca. Prayers hurriedly mumbled, the line of trucks roared onto the rutted highway again and began to move. This ancient road had been paved by the Russians during the stresses of the last war, when the whole world was galvanized to strenuous action. But the temporary film of asphalt had degenerated during the peaceful years, it had not been repaired, the sand had blown in, and now the broken remains of the paving did more harm than good. Shortly the trucks passed a long old-fashioned string of camels, which drew to one side to let them pass, the drivers exchanging simultaneous greetings of welcome and farewell;

and then the motor vehicles disappeared in a cloud of dust and noise to the north.

Like the camels the trucks traveled only at night. The sun of the Gobi Desert raises the earth's surface temperature so high it melts tires and camels develop sores on their pads. Compared with the Gobi the Sahara is a garden. Here, in certain stretches of the road, were places where rain had never fallen. There were no oases. There was no life. Neither scorpions nor jackals nor flying insects nor even insects that crawled could live under so dry, so hot a sun. It was the most totally lifeless region on the face of the planet. But traders from China had crossed it for thousands of years. It was the only way to go, and trade had to move because it connected China with Outer Mongolia and the Siberian regions to the north. Remote as it was, it had played a conspicuous part in the interchange of culture and commerce. Traditionally tea and silk flowed north along the trade route, and in the opposite direction Mongolian wool and Siberian furs flowed south. Great quantities still did, with camels carrying the freight as they had done for millennia.

But now there was an enormous traffic in rifles, machine guns, ammunition and industrial dynamite needed by the Mongol Peoples Republic and available from China. In the warehouses of Kalgan were vast quantities of old but useable war surplus left over from World War II. It bore the manufacturers' marks of all the countries which had recently fought there: England, Japan, Germany, who had written off the material because it was too distant to return profitably, and forgotten it. But the guns would still shoot, the shells would still explode, the mortars would still kill.

Now the Mongol Peoples Republic, affiliated with the USSR, needed these arms. To transport them from Kalgan to Ulan Bator trucks were faster and more efficient than camels, and many a trader bid for the contracts, now again profitable, to conduct the truck caravans.

Ahmed Timur was a state employee of the Mongol Peoples Republic and so, nominally, he was a Communist; but the state ideology conflicted with his inherited religion and was dulled by it. Only on the surface was he a Communist.

His state-fixed salary was sweetened by many bonuses and incentive payments. He saw in these prerequisites the state's need of him; and he reflected that there must be little change in the world from the days when his old father, who had been an extremely successful merchant and brigand, first took him to the mosque in Kalgan where, as a boy, he had learned that the Prophet, still living in Paradise, had also once been a successful merchant and had advocated as a good work the amassing of as large a fortune as possible in the least possible time. National states might come and go, Ahmed Timur mused; state ideologies and international loyalties shifted; but the power of Allah and gold remained firm.

"That cursed camel train, led by some son of a jackal, started a whole hour earlier than I," he growled to his driver. "They stole a march on the sunset. Infidels. Accursed. Accursed they shall be." He spat. "Who but an infidel sets out before sunset?"

"It was hard to judge the sunset tonight," his driver said. "There were two suns and circles of queer confusing light with spots of brilliance strung like pearls around the circles of light that connected them. Perhaps he made an honest mistake."

"Camel drivers are never honest. He took advantage. He cheated. In Hell his tongue will swell and burst with thirst."

"Perhaps so."

"That cursed camel-loving son of a jackal used the wrong

sun. It was only a sundog. Anybody can recognize a sundog."

"Has it occurred to you, sir, that it is unprecedented to witness a sundog in the Gobi?" He was younger than Timur and had had some schooling at Ulan Bator. "Sundogs are caused by ice in the stratosphere; ice crystals require moisture to form; there is no moisture here no matter how far up you go."

"That is true," said Ahmed Timur thoughtfully. "I have never witnessed moisture. I have never seen a drop of rain."

"But we witnessed the sundog."

"Do not say that." And yet he had witnessed the sundog.

"There will be rain."

"No!"

A few drops of pink rain splattered against the windshield. Ahmed Timur felt his spine tingle, and prayed. Next day, as they sighted the plateau of Outer Mongolia like the rim of a giant disc riding upwards against the sky, it began to snow. They were still on the fringes of the Gobi. It was against nature. The snow was pink.

CHAPTER 5

In Canadian fishing waters the captain-owner of the *Angélique*, a diesel trawler, turned off his ship-to-shore radio and grinned, and put the boat back on a course to the fishing grounds. He had got a good report from the station at Percé. The doctor said the baby would be a few more days in coming and it was not necessary to return. "I'll call you when I send her to the hospital, Narcisse. No, have no fear; everything is going just as it did nine times before." Parbleu, wouldn't one think that after nine times a man wouldn't worry?

Narcisse Bolduc had fathered nine children in ten years of marriage and another was about to be born. A new bébé always put him in a good mood.

"I am *not* worried," he said emphatically to the doctor. "I'm three-quarters' full of prime cod already. I can come in if Angélique is in labor and then make another quick trip when little Angélique is born."

"You're still sure it's going to be a girl," the doctor chuckled.

"Five of each," said Narcisse. "That will even up the score."
He had set his heart on five of each.

"A neat methodical man," said the doctor, amused. "Symmetrical in the mind. That is good. One leaves, however, something to God in matters like these. I will call you, Narcisse. Au revoir, and good fishing."

Narcisse Bolduc belonged to the new generation of full-time fishermen, wholly different from the traditional shiftless pêcheurs-nomadiques of the past, who had been little more than migrant laborers; they would log in the wintertime, fish with leaky, antiquated craft when there was nothing better to do, and drift off to menial factory jobs far from home in the summer. Narcisse Bolduc was industrious and thrifty.

He was fiercely proud of the Gaspé, its French heritage, customs and language. He had a brother who was a priest. He himself was head of the *Pêcheurs-Unis*, the United Fishermen, a cooperative organization somewhat like a labor union but far wider in scope. The *Pêcheurs-Unis* sought out markets for fish, built storage and processing plants, set up purchasing funds for buying nets, salt, fuel oil and other supplies wholesale—and, with his brother the curé to bless the boats and christen the children—tried bravely to teach the highly individualistic French-Canadian fishermen to work together, a difficult task, as anyone born into that proud and tradition-minded minority knew. He spoke some English and accepted with reluctance the fact that les anglais, as all good Gaspésians called the English-speaking Canadians to the west, still actually owned the Maritime Provinces. One had only to look at the Anglican church at Percé to realize that the English flaunted their overlordship in ways and in places where they were not wanted. But the Anglican church was a small stone building and looked like a postcard and almost nobody went there. The church of his brother the curé was big and red and brick, and on top was a beautiful tin spire that shone like gold in the sunset, and it was always full. Still, one had to be fair and give the English credit. There had come from Toronto a new quick-freezing device, a pilot model, that dehydrated, froze and reduced to one-tenth its size any fish you put into it. It did not thereafter have to be refrigerated. Weeks or months later the woman bought it off a shelf in a store and soaked it in water, it swelled up plump again, and then she cooked it and the result was almost as good as a fresh-caught fish. Yes, you had to give les anglais some credit. He had fought in the Korean War in an English-speaking Canadian division, and they were good fighters.

He called me symmetrically minded, he remembered, grinning again. And so I am when I really think about things. If I should turn back for the birth of Angélique, if le bon dieu grants me a girl, I should have only three-quarters of a load, and if I made another trip after that I would have one and three-quarters before the season ends. But if I fish till I'm full and then dash home and then make another trip I shall have two loads. Anyone knows that two loads is better than one and three-quarters. One had to work hard for an ever-growing family.

Thus emboldened he cheerfully steered out towards the fishing grounds, and ran into bad luck. Other boats had fished them dry, or perhaps the creatures had taken it into their heads to swim elsewhere, as occasionally they did for no explicable reason. He steered farther north to a bank he sometimes worked, and after a fruitless couple of days, during which he drew up a minimum of fish, he said, "So! You have all gone south, have you? You will not escape Narcisse Bolduc!" and made a long arc into Chaleurs Bay. During this

time he was out of radio range with Percé, but the hauls
were excellent and he filled the hold of the *Angélique*.

"The bébé will have been born," he reflected as he turned
the *Angélique* homeward. "But one leaves, as the doctor
said, something to God in these matters. I will kiss her and
see her christened, and then I will go back to Chaleurs Bay
and fill my hold again." He said a prayer for *Angélique*, the
boat, for Angélique his wife, and for Angélique the child, if
the Good Lord granted him a baby girl, and shut off the
motor and set the sail, since he was running short of fuel. He
had been gone longer than he anticipated. He was anxious for
news. He was still out of range of Percé. The cod were
salted, the hatches closed. Narcisse settled down and waited
impatiently for the wind to blow him home. The small crew
stowed the net and lazed about and smoked their pipes and
made bets with each other whether the bébé Bolduc would
be a boy or a girl.

That night a light appeared in the southern sky, climbed
rapidly to the zenith till the whole arch of heaven blazed
white. It cast no shadows because it seemed to come from
everywhere. The men crossed themselves and knelt on the
deck and prayed. Their faces frightened each other. They
were pale as ghosts. But whether it was their terror or some
weird colorless quality of the light they did not know nor
did they care.

"We think, Narcisse, we'd better get home quick," they
said.

He calmed them down. "It's probably just the Northern
Lights."

"In August?"

"I've seen them in August."

"So bright, so queer, so wicked?"

No, never so bright, he admitted, and admittedly the phenomenon was queer. But a light could not be wicked. Light was the first thing le bon dieu made when He created the world. His brother, the curé, had always loved the story of the Creation and often had mentioned that light was the first thing God called good. But this light had not looked good, so perhaps God had not made it.

Bolduc began to feel the fears that were terrifying his men, and he started the motor and steered for home.

He twirled the dials of his radio, hoping for mention of the light, searching the commercial channels between fruitless efforts to contact the marine operator at Percé. Perhaps he was still out of range.

The commercial channels were flooded with talk, but none of it was in French. Yet there should have been French broadcasts from Toronto and Montreal, which had powerful stations and served the Maritime Provinces. The men demanded news.

"I think there's news all right," he said. "There isn't any music, so it must be news. But it's all in English or some other foreign tongue." They none of them spoke English.

"You ought to be able to pick up Percé by now," they said. They looked accusingly at him.

"If you think I'm hiding something you're welcome to try the set," he said impatiently. "I'm doing the best I can."

"No, Narcisse, we trust you. Just go fast."

"If we go any faster we'll make less mileage and we'll run out of fuel. Then we'll be back on sail again. This is the most economical speed."

They said, "Very well, Captain." But he knew they thought he was merely saving fuel and he grew angry. They were friends of his and they always called him Narcisse except when they disagreed with his decisions, a thing that almost never happened.

He strode into the cabin and tried again to reach the marine operator at Percé. He could hear her faintly, but she would not answer his call. Her voice was high-pitched and urgent. She seemed to be repeating the same message over and over, like a tape recorder, though it was clear from her changing inflection that she was broadcasting the message live: "All boats of the fishing fleet are to return to home port at once, *repeat,* at once. This is for your own safety. Return at once, *repeat,* at once." Then her voice would click off and a blast of code would be heard on the same channel. Narcisse knew Morse Code and, of course, the slow, long-range maritime code; but he did not know what code was interrupting the Percé operator. After exasperating minutes she would return with the same order.

He wished he knew more English. He switched to the commercial channel where Ottawa could usually be heard, but there was nothing but static. Late in the night the Percé operator was relieved and a man came on. The man repeated the same message: All boats of the fishing fleet were to return to home port at once.

"That's what I'm doing!" he growled.

Next day at dawn he got an answer from Percé.

"What's all the trouble?" he demanded. He knew her well, the wife of a neighbor.

"Identify yourself, please."

"Look here, Madame Boucher, this is Narcisse Bolduc, as you know very well. Has my baby been born?"

There was a pause and she seemed to lower her voice.

"I know, Narcisse, but we're under censorship now. The military have taken over."

Taken over the maritime station at Percé? It was incredible. Why should the military take over a little station like

Percé when they had so many of their own? "Then that's why I heard all the code?"

"Yes. We're not supposed to talk about it. But everybody knows there's a war. It's awful down south, they say. It's awful everywhere. It hasn't hit us yet, though. Bring your boat home, Narcisse. How fast can you make it?"

"I'd say about forty-eight hours."

"You sound farther away than that."

"Maybe I am. It's been foggy. I haven't checked very accurately." He cut the loud speaker and switched to earphones, lowering his voice. "The men are upset. Things don't look right."

"I'd say you're more like three or four days away from the strength of your signal. That's what your signal sounds like."

"Maybe so. But I'll tell the men forty-eight hours."

"I understand. Maybe you're right. All the signals are a little queer. It's hard to judge."

"I'll tell the men forty-eight hours."

"OK. I'll have to make a report. They may mobilize the fishing fleet too."

"To fight? Fishing boats?"

"I don't really know anything for sure and I'm under censorship—I think. At least that's what they say. It's still pretty confused."

"Madame, I beg you. Is my baby born?"

She hesitated. In the present emergency it was not high-priority information. "Yes, Narcisse," she said, "a darling little girl."

"Is my wife all right?"

The operator's voice said, "Isn't she always? Of course she's all right. Congratulations, Papa-ten-times. I've got to go now. News is beginning to come through."

"Why can't I get Toronto or Montreal?"

"They're gone."

She clicked off and the blast of code came on again.

The men had clustered round the door of the cabin, listening. He switched on the loud-speaker.

"Well, you heard all I did," he said. They had other matters on their minds, personal fears, and they did not question him.

"That light was a lot of bombs," one of them said. "Atom bombs."

"I think so too."

"We're going to speed up the engine," said another, sourly, "Maybe my home's blown up."

"Percé isn't touched. You heard her say that if you were listening. I heard it."

"Well, we're going to speed up the engine before it is," the man said, and the others said, "Yes, by God!"

Bolduc said, "You're a pack of fools." But they looked ugly enough and scared enough to pitch him over the side if he objected. "Very well, messieurs mes amis, I'll do it myself. Then you'll have someone to blame."

They looked sheepish; then they cheered him. "Narcisse, you're a good fellow!"

He had re-established his authority over them and he had a notion that was important. He went to bed and slept for twenty hours, and wakened with a start. The vibration of the engine had stopped. He smiled grimly. They had gaspillé the fuel, acted the wastrel. They had improvidently thrown away their last best chance of getting home in a hurry. He heard them cursing. He heard the rattle of tackle as they rigged the sail. There was nothing he could do. There was a faint flutter of breeze from the south. It would carry them to Percé if it held. The atmosphere seemed insufferably hot, and he turned over to catch a moment's more rest. When he awoke a singularly red sunset was streaming through the open port and he heard the last weak flapping of the sail as a dead calm descended over the sea, which was an unpleasant purple and glassy smooth.

Narcisse got out of his bunk and went to the radio and tried to raise the operator at Percé. The generator had stopped with the motor, but his batteries were fully charged. She did not answer, though he knew he had power enough for her to pick up his signal. The Rock of Percé, that magnificent natural bridge from which Percé took its name, was actually visible on the horizon to the west, and behind it, dark against the sunset, the bulk of Mount Saint Anne.

It was a curious orientation. He was awake now, refreshed and alert. His position was considerably farther north than it should have been. Either the wind had been stronger while it blew, or some current with which he was not familiar had swept him far beyond the point where he should have turned in to shore.

The men were looking at the water, which had turned brown, as if there were fine mud in it. Here and there small spirals of mist arose. Narcisse let down a bucket and tested the temperature with his hand. It was oddly warm. The men were clearly unnerved and clustered round him and tested the water in their turn.

"It's hot as bath water," said one. "It's them bombs."

Narcisse rejected the thought, though it had also occurred to him.

"You heard Madame Boucher state unequivocally," he said, "that the war is nowhere near home. Did you see any bombs over the Rock? Did you see any planes? I did not. So there isn't any war near the Gaspé."

"We want to get home, Narcisse."

They were pleading now. He did not remind them that they had foolishly burned up their fuel in their wasteful demand for speed, and that the current was sweeping them ever farther to the north.

"So do I. It won't be long now. From the feel of the air we'll be getting a north wind soon. It's a good deal colder than it was. Probably that's what's causing the sea fog. That's why the water feels hot. The contrast."

They could understand that and they trusted him to be right about the wind.

"Meanwhile break out your fishing gear. We can always use a few more cod. We'll be home tomorrow." It was best to say tomorrow. "Just pull them in and dump them on the deck and salt them."

It would give them something familiar to do in unfamiliar circumstances and quiet their fears.

"The net, Narcisse?"

"Hell no. We'll get a wind any time. Hooks."

They began casting, over the side. It was not as efficient as trawling with a net, but many Gaspésians fished no other way, especially the old-timers who were slow in joining the *Pêcheurs-Unis,* and all Gaspésians knew how.

There were no cod. Not a fish struck. Then one man felt a tremendous jerk on his pole. The stiff bamboo bent. There was an enormous frothing at the end of the line, as a big fighting fish leapt and struggled against the hook.

Two men helped him steady the pole as he tried to lift it and fling the fish aboard. A sportsman would have reeled it in after playing it, but there were no reels on commercial fishermen's poles. They had no patience with such time-consuming niceties; they had to make a living.

Narcisse took a boat hook and plunged it into its forepart, hitting the gills by good luck. In the gathering darkness they drew it aboard. On the deck it still fought and opened and closed its ugly mouth.

It was a fighting tarpon, a fish that had no business in Gaspésian waters. Tarpon were hot-water fish and belonged in Florida, where rich Americans fished them for sport. They were useless for food.

Now Narcisse felt the full force of the fears that had made sheep or fools of the normal, good, average men who composed his crew. It was all he could do to keep his voice steady.

"Don't fish any more," he said. "Put up your gear." The tarpon on the deck mocked him out of glazing eyes. Narcisse liked an orderly ocean. He liked the predictable. Too much was happening at once. Now there was war again. Well, a war had been predicted for a long time, but this war was not orderly. It was doing queer things to his ocean. He could not have been more shaken if the man had hooked a sea serpent or a mermaid. A tarpon was just as unthinkable, but there it lay.

"Throw the thing overboard," he commanded. They readily did so. They too were shaken. "If we don't get a wind we'll fish tomorrow. But I expect we'll be home tomorrow."

He did not really believe it. The queer current was strong. But the men wanted desperately to believe it, so he reassured them. The night-long blaze of hideous light, the great blessing of the new baby, the new war with its mystery and peril, the outrageous tarpon—they represented a series of shocks to a man with a symmetrical mind. He grumbled inwardly, That doctor was being sarcastic. He meant "stupid," that's what he meant. Well, I may not be an intellectual, like the doctor, or a saint like my brother the curé, but I'm a damned good fisherman and I am not stupid. You don't get to be head of the *Pêcheurs-Unis* if you're stupid.

He glanced at the sky. There was no sign of wind; the vault of heaven was bleak and black. He kept the men busy for three days with fishing, and during that time they caught nothing.

Then, to the north, a veil of gray formed and bore down upon them, visible against the blacker dome of the firmament, drawing a curtain of opacity over the pale stars, blotting them out. It was much colder now. I knew it, thought Narcisse, but it was late in coming. And there's hail in it. He trimmed the sail to greet it.

It struck the becalmed *Angélique,* and even with her stubby mast and tiny spread of canvas, heavy with fish as she was, she heeled over thirty degrees, dunking her port rail for a moment before she righted. I'm a better than average judge of the weather, Narcisse thought. But never before had he miscalculated so seriously or drifted the better part of a week in waters he knew like the palm of his hand at the mercy of queer calms and queer currents. But—he sighed— the whole world was a little queer just now. The north wind, so long in coming, came at length and restored his confidence; and it blew the *Angélique* straight into harbor, where his brother, the curé, was waiting for him on the wharf.

On the wharf the brothers embraced. The rain and hail were pelting down. "Take my jacket," Narcisse said. "You're getting all wet."

"I've got my car," said the priest. "I am terribly glad you're safe."

"Sure I'm safe. How is Angélique? How is my daughter?"

"She's 'Angélique' too, all properly inscribed in the Parish Register. I christened her the day she was born."

"But Archange, I wanted to be at the christening! You knew that. Was she ill, weak? *Why?*"

Archange was a name that often amused les anglais, for

it meant "archangel"; but it was a common name on the Gaspé.

"I thought it best under the circumstances. She was born at the very beginning of the war when all the bombs were falling. They didn't fall here, of course, but we couldn't know they wouldn't."

"I knew she was born that night. That's about all I do know."

"It seems a long time ago," sighed the priest. "But of course I've been terribly busy."

"No, it's nine days, and I've spent them all on the ocean without radio contact and the ocean is crazy." He told him about the tarpon. "I felt like a man in solitary confinement. The crew were terrified. They'd have tied me up if I hadn't let them race the motor home. Of course we ran out of fuel. I don't even know who's fighting. I don't even know what side we're on."

"Oh, it's the usual two sides. The Communists and the free world."

"The whole world?"

"What's left of it, which seems to be considerable. No bombs fell after the first night. We think they're mounting a second offensive."

"Who started it?"

"That is a curious thing. Everything is curious about this war. Nobody seems to know. Communications are only just getting back to a semblance of normality, and all come from weak little-known places, except Omaha. They've got a powerful transmitter there. This sounds bad for all the big cities. The first few days Omaha divulged nothing, however. Censorship. Everything was in code; probably they were giving orders to their armies. They would also be counting to see which of their cities survived. When Russia and America began to fight England came in—actually London was obliterated simultaneously with Washington—and Canada followed and the rest of the West. I dare say the East is lined up solidly behind Russia. The missiles seem to be of a particularly virulent character. They eat up the substance of the earth like ulcers spreading in the flesh of a body. Then after a while destruction stops. One wonders why it does not continue, since the earth actually appears to burn and consume itself. Nothing is left but holes. Neither side will tell where all the bombs fell, but we know for certain that Toronto, Ottawa and Montreal are gone."

"Madame Boucher said something like that when I talked to her, but I didn't take it literally and I kept trying to pick up their broadcasts."

"She meant it literally, I'm afraid. She told me, before the military clamped down censorship, that she had heard two ship captains talking to each other in the St. Lawrence. One said, 'The Seaway is destroyed. Rockets have fallen on Detroit. Niagara Falls was hit and the river is flooding. Steer out to sea and safe water.' The other said, 'Where shall I go?' but there was no answer. Probably the first ship was atomized. The area of the Seaway must have been an important target. There was unutterable confusion the first day. There was nowhere to go, no one to give orders. Only now is there word that new governments are being set up. The word seems to be, 'Wait where you are. Do nothing. Orders will come.' Meanwhile, each community, each ship, each home, each man, is alone to work out his own salvation as best he can."

"You take it very calmly, Archange. It is the end of the world! It is Armageddon. But of course you are a priest."

"That is one of the few compensations I have in all the horror. My work is cut out for me. That is why I baptized

Angélique." He paused and chuckled. "Do you know, Narcisse, she was born with a tooth just erupting through the gums. I felt its sharp little point when I put the salt in her mouth. I can't remember that ever happening before, at least to me, though I've heard of it. She's a beautiful child with remarkably intelligent big brown eyes."

The car was nearing the neat Bolduc home. The storm continued, though the hail had changed to sleet interspersed with flakes of snow. Hail was not unheard of in August on the Gaspé, but snow was unprecedented. So was the winterlike cold that accompanied it out of the north.

"You will come in, Archange? You are cold and wet. You could do with a glass of wine to celebrate my homecoming to my Angélique."

The priest hesitated, looked at his watch. He knew he shouldn't, but he wanted to. His teeth were chattering. "It is after midnight," he said slowly. "There will be a sheaf of calls on my desk. I really ought not to. But I got up at four, I've had a long day and I'm due for another tomorrow. People are understandably restless. Yes, I'll come in for a moment."

"Even a curé cannot work twenty-four hours a day," Narcisse said. "You can tend to the calls tomorrow."

The house had been dark when the car entered the driveway. Now a light was turned on and the front door opened. Narcisse saw Angélique hastily tidying her hair and knotting the cord of her dressing gown. She called, "Monsieur le curé? Père Archange? I recognized your tires. But you can't come in. I'm not dressed. Have you word of Narcisse?"

"I have Narcisse himself."

"She was terribly worried," he whispered to Narcisse.

"Narcisse?"

Her welcoming little shriek was like music and Narcisse

Bolduc stuck out his chest with pride and kissed her where she stood.

"Narcisse, in front of a curé!"

"He's only a brother-in-law, Angélique." He laughed and hugged her again, while Archange looked on and smiled benignly. "Give him a glass of wine, and me too. It's bitterly cold and he's got to work tomorrow. Show me the baby. I hear she's got a tooth. You've lost a lot of weight, Angélique. Right here."

"Narcisse, you're impossible." She hurried into the bedroom and slipped on a house dress and then went to the kitchen and got the wine. At the door of the living room she paused. The priest was looking intently at his hands, his brow furrowed in perplexity. His hands were oddly pink. Narcisse was advancing towards her. His face, where she kissed it, was streaked with red.

"Narcisse, are you hurt? You look bloody."

"Huh?" he said.

"It must be something about the snow," the curé said, sighing. "Whatever it is, we'd better wash it off."

They washed themselves with soap in the big sink in the kitchen.

"There hasn't been any fallout so far," the curé said. "That's been one of the anomalies of the situation. So many bombs and no fallout. If this is the beginning I suppose it's too late to do much about it. But wash it all carefully down the sink, and I'd burn the towels if I were you because of the children. Angélique had better wash her hands and face too."

"I certainly will!" Angélique said. They heard her crying in the kitchen, and shortly the range began to roar. She had dowsed the towels with kerosene and burned them up. She returned pale and shaken.

Archange sipped his wine, glancing at the windows where

falling sleet occasionally rattled, blown by a gust of wind as if it were winter.

"After the first day," he said soberly, "we began to notice a perceptible rise in the temperature of the sea. It's been progressively hotter ever since. I'm no expert, but I dare say it's the Gulf Stream."

"Yes, it flows close."

"That would explain the tarpon, Narcisse. I'm afraid I haven't told you the worst. I couldn't believe it myself at first, but it's pretty well authenticated by now. All Central America is gone, burned up by the bombs. The Gulf Stream would naturally get pretty hot, even this far away. It will of course cool down in time, now that the bombs have stopped."

"If they don't start falling again," Angélique said.

"But I am quite at a loss to explain this storm tonight. So much is unexplainable." He sighed heavily.

It was too much for Narcisse to take in all at once. There were too many mysteries. He liked things explained to him in positive terms.

"You had better stay the night, Archange," he said. "If this keeps up, the roads will be slippery."

"I'll be needed tomorrow," the curé said. "The people will be terrified at this new phenomenon. I'll go now while I know I'll get through. Pray God it isn't fallout. It will be tested tomorrow. There's a Geiger counter in Percé now. We are quite advanced, you see. Far too advanced, in my humble opinion. I'll call you as soon as I know, Narcisse. Meanwhile, don't venture out till the storm stops. Good night, mon frère. Good night, ma soeur." Gingerly, touching nothing but the doorknob, he walked out into the pink snow.

"Your brother is a brave man," Angélique said. "I never

respected him so much as I do at this moment. He didn't want to contaminate us."

"If we're contaminated it's happened already," Narcisse said miserably. "I am and you are, and I did it. We mustn't touch the children."

"How can we help it? They'll have to be bathed and fed and put to bed and just *everything*."

"The big ones can do it for the little ones."

"For a time, I suppose," Angélique said thoughtfully, "till we run out of food in the house. Then what?"

"Then I'll go out and get more and wrap it up in an oilskin and bring it home."

"Narcisse, I think you would." She put her arms around him and kissed him.

"Hey, wait! I might be—"

"Contaminated? Then I am too. You just said so. So there's no harm, is there?"

"No, I guess not." But he felt like a leper.

"Maybe I could just take a peek at Angélique," he suggested. "Where is she?"

"In the cradle in our bedroom. They're all in there, except the big ones. She's adorable, Narcisse."

"I promise I won't touch her. Let Archange bring her in, or one of the big girls." Archange was the eldest son, named for his uncle, the curé.

"They'd hug you and kiss you, Narcisse," she said dubiously.

"Mon dieu, so they would. For God's sake, don't waken them. Let them sleep." He looked longingly towards the bedroom.

"I don't suppose there would be any harm going in just to look at her," Angélique said. "You've got to sleep in there anyhow."

"I'd planned to sleep on the floor in the living room," Narcisse said.

"I think *not*," Angélique said.

It was the first good laugh they had had since Angélique had noticed the red streaks on his face.

"I won't even touch the door," he said, tiptoeing into the bedroom.

"Neither will I."

Without thinking, Angélique snapped on the light.

"Oh dear," she said ruefully, looking at the switch. "Now that's contaminated."

"It isn't as if she could walk," Narcisse said, "but we'll have to warn the others to stay away from it." It occurred to him that through carelessness or absolute necessity there would shortly be no place in the house where nine children could go. The bathroom presented particular problems, and there was only one.

Angélique looked up out of her cradle and smiled at her mother and gurgled contentedly.

"She looks as if she knew you," Narcisse said. "She is beautiful, isn't she? She has your hair. I hope it stays blonde."

"But your eyes. Look how brown."

"Yes, they're brown all right. She's not a bit wrinkled or puckered like some of the others were."

"Good heavens, she's over a week old."

"Was she wrinkled at first?"

"Well, no; she wasn't actually."

"She's adorable," he said. It was almost impossible not to pick her up, as he had done all the others, but he actually took a step backward so as not even to breathe on her. His face was wrathful. "I could always pick up the others," he said, and swore. "But even if it's fallout, the radioactivity only lasts two weeks. We can manage not touching things for two weeks. If it ever stops snowing."

Suddenly the telephone rang. It was another object to touch. Narcisse now remembered that his shoes were damp. He had left invisible tracks of moisture all the way from the living room to the bedroom. The children must be warned not to walk anywhere barefoot, neither in the living room nor in the kitchen nor in their parents' bedroom. And they must not touch the bottom of their shoes with their fingers.

They looked at each other inquiringly as the telephone continued to ring. "I don't suppose it matters which one of us answers it," Angélique said.

"I suppose not. I'll paint everything red tomorrow that mustn't be touched. Then even the little ones who can't read will know."

Angélique answered the phone. She gave a happy cry. "Narcisse! It's all right! It's Archange. He wants to talk to you."

"What's all right?" It had been a long time since anything was all right. He picked up the phone. "Well?"

His brother's voice came strong and elated. "They've already tested it, Narcisse! There's not a trace of radioactivity. Nobody knows what it is, but it's not fallout. There's more radioactivity in the dial of your wristwatch than there is in this stuff."

"Maybe the Geiger counter doesn't work."

"They thought of that. It works all right. They tested that too. But there's more. People are scared out of their wits by this pink rain. There's a lot more farther north, and it's heavier. Messages came in from everywhere asking what it was, what to do about it. Omaha began to broadcast in the clear, no code, in half-a-dozen different languages. Madame Boucher picked it up in French at the station. There is absolutely no danger. Whatever it is, it can't hurt you. Now go kiss your little Angélique. I know what you've been thinking. Au revoir, mon vieux. I'm going to call some of the rest of my timorous flock and tell them to stop worrying about innocuous meteorological phenomena." He hung up. Narcisse could hear him laughing till the receiver clicked down and severed the connection.

"I'd have thought he was drunk if I didn't know him so well," Narcisse told Angélique, "and I don't think the good Lord would blame him if he was. He'll be on the phone till morning, reassuring everybody in the parish who has a phone. He hasn't called me 'old boy' since we were kids."

He went back to the bedroom and picked Angélique out of her cradle, suporting her head in the way that even a father becomes expert at after ten times. "Now, little lady, you're going to give your noncontaminated daddy a nice noncontaminating kiss," and he kissed her on the mouth and cheeks and stroked her hair. The fineness of babies' hair always amazed him, but Angélique's seemed the softest, silkiest, finest yet. The baby looked at him and gurgled and smiled, and there, sure enough, was a sharp little tooth point just peeking out of the pink upper gum. "That'll cause you trouble before too long," he said, looking at his wife, grinning. "You never had *that* to contend with before."

"You're an obscene sailorman," Angélique said, laughing. "You don't know what you're talking about. I've heard of it before. They don't bite you, you know."

"How in the world would I know?" he said. Then, turning again to the baby, "Now give your nice obscene daddy back his kiss."

Little Angélique pursed her lips and smiled again.

"You are entirely too sophisticated for a ten-day old," Narcisse said. "Never kiss a sailorman the first time he asks you.

You are not *angélique;* you are *diabolique.* You are a bad girl."

The baby began to cry.

"For goodness' sake, Narcisse, you're frightening her. She was only swallowing when she made that little moue. Give her to me."

Narcisse laughed and relinquished the bundle, which promptly gurgled and went to sleep in its mother's arms.

Angélique put her back into the cradle.

"She doesn't know you yet," she said reproachfully.

"Of course not. How could she in ten days? They don't know anything that early. So she didn't know what I was talking about, and I'm sorry if I scared her making faces at her. Now let's wake up the others so I can see them."

He often did that on returning from a trip.

Angélique said doubtfully, "It's nearly morning. Wouldn't it be better to let them sleep? Then we'll all have a big family breakfast."

"Madame Bolduc," he said after perhaps a full second's thought, "it's no wonder we have so many children."

CHAPTER 6

In Jamaica the fog and hot weather quickly passed. Bill and Betty Young drove up from Las Palmas to their cottage on the mountainside. "As a rule we would keep you here a week," the doctor said. "But in the present uncertain state of affairs we're emptying all the beds we can because we can't tell when they'll be needed. I feel better about discharging you early than any other mother I ever sent home. Your recovery was so quick I can only compare it with the primitives, who would take a few hours off to have their babies, then catch up with the caravan and take their place with the newborn on their backs as if nothing had happened. If all mothers were so healthy we doctors would soon be out of business."

Betty smiled. "It's certainly something to be a primitive, isn't it?"

"I'm afraid I said it wrong," the doctor said.

"But it really is nice to be told I'm healthy."

She did not hold it against him that his praise was not very diplomatic. Probably the best doctors had the worst bedside manner.

As for Wilson Young, Jr., he somewhat bewildered the doctor. He was curiously precocious in his development. Except for his normal size he looked and reacted like a six-months-old infant. He had, in his first four days, cut two upper incisor teeth, and the lower ones were visible under the gums.

"A fine, strong baby, Mrs. Young. Not a thing to worry about. Absolutely normal, and one of the handsomest I've seen." Betty beamed. But he felt he ought to reassure her about the early eruption of the teeth.

"Many children are born with them, Mrs. Young," he said when she asked if it wasn't unusual. "It's nothing to cause you the least bit of concern."

CHAPTER 7

DURING the undeclared truce while communications were being improvised, reports began to filter in to the heads of the provisional governments, while both sides jockeyed for positions of military advantage. There were ominous and perplexing phenomena. In the final resolution, as is now well known, they formed a cohesive inevitable whole; but at the time they were treated as military secrets. How the term "cold war" rang in the ears of the military! But before long the military played a decreasing role in the decisions that had to be made. The war was still on, but it became a different war. Still war, but what a war and against what a foe! And still cold—how infinitely colder than anyone had ever imagined. In the united effort that supervened, the military became subordinate to the scientists, especially the meteorologists and the engineers.

Everywhere in the northern latitudes the unseasonable cold continued, and precipitation, which was pink at first, came down; sometimes as rain, sometimes as sleet, most often as snow.

There were other anomalies. The Distance Early Warning

Lines across the tundras of Canada were not hit by the missiles. Their mission was to warn Washington of imminent attack. But since, within seconds, there would be no Washington to warn, it was not thought worthwhile to waste nuclear material on them. Thus they continued to function throughout the entire Twenty Minute War, but actually they had no function because Washington was already a hole in the ground. Then, from Omaha, orders went out to the DEW Lines, orders signed by generals whose names they did not know, confirmed by a Chief of Staff they had never heard of. The orders, urgent, hurried, read, "Withdraw. Abandon Stations." The disciplined personnel obeyed, following pre-prepared evacuation plans, which were detailed and minute. But the Distance Early Warning Lines were intimately meshed with a transportation system that had ever-decreasing supply bases to the rear, all verging on a few big Canadian cities. None of the actual stations had long range planes nor the great fields required for 5000-mile aircraft. The personnel evacuated indeed, but they flew to burnt-out rear bases that had been atomized, and perished in the snow.

There were tragedies that struck down whole peoples, whose names were almost unknown. There were the Koryaks of Kamchatka. They were a primitive Mongol tribe on the Russian side of the northern Pacific. They were already debilitated by the white man's importations of syphilis, smallpox, measles and alcoholism. Now came The Twenty Minute War, another white man's gift, with its change in the weather. This small people, whose extinction was fated to occur anyhow, had always been subject to a strange affliction called "Arctic Hysteria." No scientist, whether medical or sociological, had ever discovered its cause. It was called "Arctic" because it struck them during the long Arctic nights; but not all Arctic peoples were prey to it and many dwellers in Tropical zones suffered similar maladies, characterized by sudden disorientation and bursts of ferocity during which persons of any age or sex, but usually men, went wild and killed anything that moved.

The Koryaks of Kamchatka never lived to celebrate their Fawn Festival. They looked up at the falling pink snow, which in Kamchatka was very heavy, and went mad. Arctic Hysteria, isolation, a primitive culture in a region without transportation brought sickness and slow starvation, and ultimately freezing exterminated them all.

On the American side of the Pacific were the Aleuts. They too died in their isolated villages, cut off from a world that no longer could send ships or planes to supply them with the necessities of life. All around the globe a similar fate fell upon the Eskimos who lived on the circumpolar shores that fringe the Arctic Ocean. In their trading posts supplies ran out. Generators stopped for lack of gasoline. Then there was no oil for even a lantern. They remembered their stone lamps with moss wicks and blubber grease, but hunger reduced them to eating the blubber. They fished for more, but walruses, seals and even the seagulls, all had disappeared, warned by the same immemorial racial memory that all was not well with the weather, too much cold had come too early, and survival lay to the south. Bereft of the food fauna that traditionally sustained them, frantically the Eskimos built igloos, in summer, and died, marveling at the pink ice.

Deaths of great multitudes not counted in the two hundred million casualties directly caused by the missiles were not confined to the extreme northern latitudes. In Tibet, Switzerland, everywhere the land was high, insidiously and inexorably came The Big Ice. It was not at first actual ice. It began as a persistent snowfall that later compacted into ice. The lowest stratum was pink, fading gradually to normal white as it continued to pile up. None of it was radioactive at any time, proof of the cleanliness of the bombs and reason for their astounding efficiency.

The wind patterns changed also. High-flying reconnaissance planes reported that the Jet Stream was contracting towards the equator. Meteorological planes went aloft to confirm or deny the report, and confirmed it.

At lower levels where the winds touch the surface of the earth the prevailing westerlies dropped ten degrees south of their normal course, bringing with them their moisture and storms. Grass appeared in the Sahara, and it was remembered that North Africa had once been the granary of the Roman Empire, which fell when it desiccated.

It was as if a giant vise had been clamped on the poles of the planet, crushing everything it touched and forcing life to flee before it into a progressively narrowing zone in the torrid belt of the earth. In the first weeks of The Pause, before these complex changes were understood, each community was conscious only of its own personal loss and the local change of weather.

CHAPTER 8

In Magnitogorsk in the Metal Workers Palace the (provisional) Supreme Soviet assembled every day in permanent emergency session. In Omaha, in the underground shelter that had been kept as secret as the Manhattan Project of World War II the (provisional) Congress of the United States was also meeting. In both parliamentary bodies it was noticed that each day fewer and fewer members of the military were present, either as members or advisors.

On both sides the reason for their absence was the same: their first duty was to extricate their armies and bring them back from all the far-flung thousands of secret bases where they were now stationed and which were now threatened not by enemy missiles but by an unstoppable planetary snowfall. On both sides it was a Dunkirk evacuation, but the enemy was climate, a climate horribly mutilated by war. Both sides still planned to continue the war if conditions became more favorable. But they never did, and presently the armies were employed in a task no less arduous than battle, as were indeed the civilian populations of the whole world.

In the absence of the military and step by step with reports of continuing snowfall in the higher latitudes, members of both parliaments began to demand explanations and, above all, "How long will it last?"

Speaking in Magnitogorsk, Academician Anapolskoi answered, "It will last till the Isthmus of Panama is replaced."

A new, very scared member cried, "Where is it? We thought it was gone. We'll replace it." She was a hefty, willing Coordinator of Collective Farms in the Ukraine who had been chosen because she had risen to prominence in her own limited sphere and believed nothing was impossible.

A better informed member shouted, "How can you rebuild seven hundred miles of pulverized earth?"

Anapolskoi paid no attention to the interruptions. "I do not know," he said, "but unless we rebuild it, conditions will get worse."

There was a time, he told them, when the Isthmus of Panama did not exist, a rather recent time, geologically speaking. The Rocky Mountains and the Andes are very young. Panama is simply the top of a continuous range that stretches from Cape Horn to Bering Strait, from Antarctica to the Arctic Ocean, forming a dam against the natural flow of ocean currents around the world.

In the tropical Atlantic a river of hot water flows from east to west. Its motion is due to the winds and to water's inertia, both caused by the planet's rotation. But for the damming action of the slender strip of Central America it would flow unimpeded around the globe as it did in glacial times. This is the Gulf Stream.

In the Pacific there is likewise a river of water, but this river is cold and has its origin in the Antarctic. This is the Humboldt Current.

"That dam has proved of great value to man," Anapolskoi

said. "It is not, perhaps, too much to say that that dam has made man what he is today. The present climate difficulty is owing to the fact that the dam no longer exists, and the Gulf Stream accordingly flows unimpeded around the world as it did before man evolved, dissipating its warmth in the cold of the Humboldt Current.

"Man himself has effectively destroyed the God-given geological formation that quite likely raised him above the brutes and wrought in him the capacity to reason.

"Striking the Isthmus of Panama, during the eons while it was permitted to remain there, the Gulf Stream was deflected north, warming the American coasts as far north as Labrador, fanning out in a beneficent flow and crossing over to Europe, thus rendering Europe temperate and habitable. Only after that dam, now lost, arose from the sea bottom did the northern glaciers retreat and man appear. It is possible that they will readvance and man disappear. There is considerable evidence to support such a thesis."

No one interrupted him now, not even when he made reference to God, and he continued with the detachment that characterized him when he lectured before the Academy.

For a short while, he said, the Gulf Stream had flowed on of its own momentum in its accustomed course. Heated while Panama was burning, it superheated the Atlantic Coast of North America to the latitude of the Gaspé Peninsula and, after crossing the Atlantic, brought fog, rain and sweltering hot weather to Europe.

It was replaced by an enormous "upwelling" of icy polar water. This was a current that normally flows sluggishly out of the Arctic Ocean, along the ocean floor, from the North Pole to the equator. The Gulf Stream, being warm and of less specific gravity, flowed over it. Now the Gulf Stream no longer existed. Hence the Atlantic was not only bereft of its warmth, with all its blessings to Europe and America, but the condition was actually made worse by the upwelling of this polar water.

There were angry shouts, "Anapolskoi says we are doomed!"

Anapolskoi shrugged. "The multiplicity of individual man and the dispersion of his habitat render him ineradicable simultaneously, so it can be assumed that some of us will survive to eke out a primitive existence in the tropics, if we can get there in time. I am not an expert in rapid transit. The oceans I love and have made my study move slowly. I must leave the logistics of the mass migration of whole peoples to transportation engineers."

He was frightening them. Someone screamed, "Are we all going to die?"

Anapolskoi said, "I shouldn't think so. A colleague of mine is in the rhododendron forests of Tibet, an anthropologist. I do not expect to see him again, since Tibet is very high and everyone there must be dead. But he wrote me before the war that he had come across traces of a being which he believed to be the degenerate remnant of Neanderthal Man. You will have heard of the *yeti,* which the English call the Abominable Snowman. It was my colleague's belief that the *yeti* adjusted to the glacial age and survived it. It is an interesting hypothesis."

As Anapolskoi, who was fatigued and disheartened, gathered up his notes and was about to leave the podium, there was a cry, "We will rebuild the Isthmus of Panama!" It was followed by roars of applause, in which Anapolskoi detected a distinct undertone of hysteria.

"That would be still more interesting. It probably *could* be done," he agreed dubiously, "if the Americans, the British, if all our enemies and all our friends, if everybody united in the work."

As The Pause lengthened, as no more bombs fell, as more information was gathered and the enormity of the menace of The Big Ice became ever more apparent, there were cautious peace feelers on both sides between the provisional governments of East and West. Each wanted to know if the other was experiencing the same climatic change, its extent and locality. All this had been muffled by censorship at first. Each conceded that there had been certain odd happenings.

Then, as the peril mounted, each agreed to exchange representatives. Traditionally they would have met in Geneva; but Geneva, being situated at a high altitude, was under three feet of snow, the airfield unusable, and throughout Switzerland all those who could were migrating to Italy. In the Alpine valleys many had starved. Many more starved in trains that stalled in the drifts and were wrecked when they ran through switches that switchmen had deserted.

Time was pressing. In an unprecedented emergency each side agreed to an unprecedented departure from protocol: they agreed to send their representatives directly to each other's capital under a flag of truce, painted plainly on the wings and bodies of the aircraft.

Simultaneously two giant jets arose from Omaha and Magnitogorsk and arrived the same day in their enemy's heartland. Over the Atlantic the planes spotted each other on their radar, and each changed course so as not to pass close, each fearing a homing missile: the war was still on. It would confer a distinct advantage on the side which first shot down the other's scientists and political plenipotentiaries. But neither plane fired.

In the Russian plane the negotiators talked nervously

among themselves. "Since the Americans did not shoot us down in mid-ocean it may be that there was no one in their plane, that it was simply a disguised missile on its way to destroy Magnitogorsk."

"Equally they may think," Anapolskoi said, "that we are an unmanned missile on our way to destroy Omaha. I'm afraid we shall have to trust each other." He pointed to the whiteness below.

They had seen the devastation of Russia. The Urals were an unrelieved spine of blue ice two hundred miles wide, stretching north and south as far as the eye could see. From the Urals to Scandinavia the great Russian plain was blanketed with snow. Far to the north it was blue-white; to the south where it was thinner, it was still the mysterious pink of the first fall. Over Kazan there was smoke coming out of the municipal utility chimneys. Kazan had not been hit. The plane picked up the Kazan radio station, which was broadcasting instructions to the surrounding area: refugees were being warned that rail transportation to the south was disrupted; those wishing to migrate to the still-temperate shores of the Black Sea were urged to organize caravans of wheeled vehicles with wide-tread tires and supply themselves with food, warm clothing and shovels, and to keep to the roads, avoiding the bombed cities. Danger lurked around the great holes where the cities had been; it was not an atomic danger; it was the survivors. Far beyond the actual crater areas, a mantle of devastation spread over the land where virtually everything edible and wearable had been burned or blown to pieces by hurricane-force winds. Still there were many who, by a twist of fate or a miracle of accident, had been in some sheltered spot and escaped injury. These were now banding together like locusts. Many were armed and all were hungry.

Beyond Kazan was a crater that had been Gorki, and
westward of Gorki was the largest crater of all. Here had
been Moscow, and a concentration of missiles had fallen.

The Scandinavian Peninsula was as blue as the Urals and
its fjords were beginning to clog with ice.

Then they witnessed the devastation of America. From
Newfoundland, which was white, to the latitude of Detroit,
where the snow was thin and pink, the Russian scenes were
repeated: there were craters where Montreal, Toronto, Boston, New York, Buffalo, Pittsburgh, Cleveland, Detroit and
Chicago had been.

"Now I am sure we can trust them," Anapolskoi reassured
his colleagues. "It would be totally illogical to add one more
bomb to all this. It would add no more to the damage than a
single raindrop adds to the bulk of the sea. The Americans
may not be cordial but assuredly they will not be hostile,
since they will have had reports from their plane about conditions in Russia. All over the world it must be the same.
What will they do? I do not know. What can anyone do
now?"

In Magnitogorsk and in Omaha the negotiators landed and
exchanged information, reluctantly at first but more fully
as observations on each side were compared with the other's
and found to be accurate. All over the northern hemisphere
the same dire climatic change was taking place. The Americans, being closer to the scene of the Panama catastrophe,
had reached the same diagnosis of the cause as Academician
Anapolskoi, namely, the disappearance of what had been
known as the Gulf Stream, and the new course of the warm
current, still warm, but now flooding into the Pacific.

With the whole world a shambles, The Pause gave promise of permanence, since all who survived The Twenty Min-

ute War were called upon to fight not an ideology but something more cosmic: The Big Ice. In all the negotiations there was only one smile: A Russian negotiator, in a tedious speech, permitted himself a good deal of abusive rhetoric on the evils of nuclear weapons. "If you people had not invented the things," he said, "we would not all find ourselves in this common predicament." An American arose to thank him for giving America credit for one invention.

When it was seen that the Russians and Americans could meet and confer in good faith on the climatic change and search for remedial measures, scientists from other nations were called to Omaha to help. Many men with great names were missing; they had been atomized. But there were many whom chance had spared, and they came to the councils.

There was more to The Big Ice than the loss of the Gulf Stream. A prominent Italian volcanist, with a scar on his face where Stromboli had seared him with lava, explained it.

Another physical law, he said, was also working towards and actually speeding a man-made glacial age. When Central America blew up, along with the Saint Lawrence Seaway and other critical targets, an enormous quantity of matter was burned. It oxidized and was hurtled into the stratosphere. The stuff that had once been earth and rock and animal and vegetable life had been reduced to colloidal dust, burned in incredible heat and greatly simplified in structure. It was lighter in weight than the lightest ash and almost molecular in fineness. It now floated like a pall in the upper atmosphere. In time it would filter down under the pull of gravity, starting with the heavier particles, but not all of it for many years. Meanwhile it would act like a curtain, cutting off some of the light of the sun. Any darkening of the sun is serious, since the globe's body temperature is precariously balanced, and the present darkening was sufficient to be noticeable. The dust now floating in the upper air, therefore, was another factor adding to the cold.

There remained, however, one oddity: Why was the first rain red? Why was the first snow pink? This too was explained, and some of the terror was lifted from minds that saw in it a mantle of blood spreading over the world and from eyes that looked up and saw the moon in a ruddy mist and envisioned the end of the world and the consummation of the Bible prophesy, "the sun became black as sackcloth of hair, and the moon became as blood." The explanation came from the World Meteorological Organization, before it ceased to function. This extremely valuable but little known body was a concept of the United Nations with headquarters at Geneva. Once it had had eight thousand stations all over the world which sent it their local weather information. Its corps of meteorologists digested, analyzed, charted and broadcast worldwide weather reports each day, utilizing not only its substations' information but checking their charts against television pictures received from the complex of Tiros satellites. In the havoc caused by The Twenty Minute War thousands of the WMO ground stations disappeared, but those that remained, plus the weather satellites, reported red rain and pink snow, a phenomenon that shortly occurred in Geneva itself. Geneva was soon in danger of permanent isolation, but before the personnel of the WMO fled for their lives to lower altitudes and the warmth of Italy they analyzed the red "fallout."

From the radiological point of view it was harmless, but from the point of view of precipitation it was deadly. The heavier particles of the dust in the air were the first to filter down. On analysis they were found to be tinged with iron oxide. Round these red impalpable nuclei, following a natural physical law, moisture formed. In an atmosphere saturated with water vapor, owing to the boiling of the sea, the heavy precipitation of fog, rain, sleet, hail and snow began, grew in volume and remained, laying an insulating blanket upon the earth and stretching an insulating veil through the atmosphere, intensifying the cold. Through man's loosing of these synergetic forces was brought on the awesome accident of The Big Ice, which added its toll of death by starvation, cannibalism, madness and freezing to the deaths of The Twenty Minute War.

Earth would abide, but whether man, at least in his present form, would survive was for some time debatable.

Then, faced with common extinction, laying aside the conflicting ideologies and the viciousness with which they had mangled each other, the two sides joined hands in the biggest engineering project ever devised by the temperamental and extremely ingenious mentality of Homo Sapiens. He had built pyramids in Egypt, no light undertaking for those times, to save his soul. Now he decided to rebuild the Isthmus of Panama to save his life. The reconstituted dam stands today as man's ultimate achievement. No being endowed with such compulsive and imaginative will-to-live must ever be deemed mere animal. His potential is prodigious. In the reading of this history all true men will bear their proud heritage in mind.

CHAPTER 9

In Percé on the Gaspé the precipitation was without letup. The snow had lost its pinkish tinge and now fell pure white, alternating with sleet and hailstones, some of them big as baseballs. It had melted at first on the ground, which was still warm from the summer sun and the hot water that had washed the peninsula for ten days. Then the sea turned cold and the sun was invisible above the clouds. Wintry winds blew from the north and arctic birds appeared on L'Ile Bonaventure, a bird sanctuary, and chased the accustomed denizens away, fighting them fiercely and eating the half-formed young that as yet had not learned to fly. Birds are never cannibals if they can find easier food, in their case fish; but the fish too, with the winds, had gone south. The cold sea, upwelling from the deep Arctic Current, was hostile, sterile, empty.

Like the birds, like the fish, though slower because instinct guided them less directly than the lower orders of life, the people of the Gaspé fled before the menace and migrated towards the south. The decision to evacuate their homes seemed to strike them simultaneously. One day they said,

116

"It will pass; we will stay." And the next day they were clamoring for space on planes, trains, trucks, ships, anything that would move.

Narcisse Bolduc did not join the refugees who took the overland escape routes. His weather sense warned him that this was a snowfall that would not melt and would not stop. He judged from the persistence of clouds and increasing cold that trains and other wheeled vehicles would not get through. There were not enough planes for everyone; planes now landed less and less often at Percé; the price of space had soared and the rich had already bought up all the seats.

He walked up the pilgrim trail to the summit of Mount Saint Anne to see how the weather looked from the normally cooler height. It looked bad. The Grand Crevasse was filled with snow. The waterfalls were frozen. His brother, the curé, was there at the head of a small group of frightened old women and men, leading a prayer of intercession at the foot of the cross that topped the shrine. Archange turned toward him and smiled, without interrupting his prayers, and blessed him, greeting him as if he were one of the pilgrims. Narcisse knew he was expected to kneel, and for a moment he did, murmuring to himself not a prayer but a mental surrender for the pilgrims, "These poor old souls will never get out. They haven't got the means. They haven't the strength." Shortly he rose from his knees and slipped away, feeling oddly guilty, glad when the slow-falling snow hid his retreating figure. "But no one saw me go," he said. But he knew his brother had seen him. "He hasn't ten children!" he growled, and put out of his mind the answer he knew Archange would have spoken to that.

He was chilled to the bone after the long descent from Mount Saint Anne. He stopped at his home to get warm before continuing on to what he had next in mind. Angélique met him at the door with a curious expression on her face.

"I hope I did nothing wrong," she said. "I couldn't help what I did."

"What did you do?" He looked around. The house looked normal. The children were eating supper, normal and noisy as usual. The cottage was cozy and warm.

"The Peckhams came by in their car, the whole family. They're going south."

That would be George and Nancy Peckham, Narcisse thought, and their two children, an Anglican family the Bolducs scarcely knew.

"They weren't able to buy supplies in the store, though I know there's plenty there. But you know, the Peckhams are English."

Narcisse smiled, "I know. So you raided the pantry. No?"

"Well, I gave them all I could."

"You didn't do wrong, Angélique."

"Everything is so odd nowadays. I hoped you wouldn't mind."

It turned out that Angélique had given them about twenty pounds of canned goods and some fresh meat.

"You probably saved their lives. I'm glad you did. But don't do it again when the next one comes begging." In his heart Narcisse did not believe Angélique had saved their lives, only prolonged their agony. Somewhere the Peckhams would get caught in a snowdrift when their old car ran out of gas, and the food would be stolen from their frozen bodies. He did not tell Angélique.

"I'm going down to take a look at the boat," he said.

"But you haven't had your supper."

"I'll have it when I come back. Keep it on the stove."

"The gas pressure's a little low," she said. "They've begun to ration it. I'm afraid of an explosion."

"Then I'll eat it cold."

"I'll put it on the electric plate," she said.

He glanced at the lights. They were still bright. It was a comforting sign. The panic was not yet too widespread.

"Good," he said. "Better not use the gas from now on."

"Electricity's terribly expensive to cook on," she said, "and you can't make a meal for twelve on one little hot plate."

"We won't be needing it much longer," he said.

"Will we be going, too?" she said, looking at the children. "Is it really so bad?"

He shrugged, "Yes, by God, we're going. But tell everybody we're staying right here, tell them there isn't the slightest danger."

She shivered a little as he put on his oilskin and went out the door, through which the slow, persistent snow drifted in. Under his big fisherman's waterproof she saw an unaccustomed bulge. He was hiding the shotgun.

At the wharf of the *Pêcheurs-Unis* the *Angélique* lay staunch and secure, riding on a gentle swell and making a well-remembered comfortable crunch as she nudged against the fenders. Narcisse had woven them himself out of sound parts of spare lines and stuffed them with lumps of old cork from life preservers he no longer considered sufficiently buoyant. He disliked fishermen who let their boats scrape against the piles. It was slipshod, it wasn't neat, and in the end it cost you money for new paint.

He stared at the sea for an instant and scowled. Its color had changed. Gone was the warm, ruddy remnant of the Gulf Stream. This water was distinctly whitish in color, like a mountain lake that owes its existence to the melting of a glacier. He tasted it. It seemed less salt.

He went aboard and listened to the radio. He had heard Madame Boucher attempting to contact ships that were steaming out of the St. Lawrence, begging them to put in at Percé if only for a few hours. "There are thousands of refugees—" Then she corrected herself and Bolduc knew that she was afraid she would frighten them with her mention of thousands. He thought with a chill that there probably *were* thousands converging from the farms in the hinterland by now, seeking sea transport away to the south. "There are only a few in this little town," Madame Boucher said, "but they are frightened and they want to get away. They are honest simple people and they have money to pay their passage."

If a single one answers, thought Narcisse, I'll try to help too. It was a sort of test. He could see the smoke of several ships on the horizon within twenty miles of Percé. Not one answered.

A crisp military voice broke in on Madame Boucher's frequency. "Percé, you are off schedule. Percé, your channel must not be used till 0400. Percé, shut down. You will be evacuated according to schedule. Percé, shut down. Shut down or we will come in and dismantle you." The voice identified itself and the name of the ship. It was urgent, but not unkind. Yet it was full of authority. Narcisse judged it must come from the nearest smoke, which had under it a ship that looked like a destroyer.

Narcisse scowled. "I'd like to know when 'according to schedule' is," he said. He knew it would not be soon enough.

In his cabin there was a high-powered rifle on a rack over his bunk. He used it to kill sharks when they scared the cod or threatened his nets and because he disliked sharks on principle. He took it down from the rack and padlocked it in the compartment under his bunk. He checked his ammunition, and wished he had more. He glanced at the fuel gauge and noted with satisfaction that it registered full. He was glad he had filled the tank the moment he returned. He did not at first look in the sail locker; he knew the sail was good because he had so recently used it. Then he did look to be sure it was there, and of course it was. He searched for a spare padlock and padlocked the sail locker too. All around him other fishing boats rode quietly alongside the wharves. No one was standing watch on them; no one was molesting them. "Not yet," he thought.

The shotgun might cause comment under his oilskin, so he locked it away with the rifle and went ashore. There's no use panicking people, he thought grimly.

He went home and ate his supper.

"We'd better replace those supplies tomorrow," he said to Angélique.

She looked at him queerly. "The stores are keeping open till nine," she said. "Everybody's buying up everything. The merchants say they never had so much business. It's like a run on a bank."

"Already?"

"That's what they say. I called up to order some things."

"I'll stock up now," he said.

"Narcisse, when are we leaving?"

"I'll tell you when I come back."

"How are we going? The car?"

"The *Angélique*. Don't let the kids know yet. They'd want to take all their friends."

"So do I."

"I do too, dear. We'll see."

In Percé village it looked like a week end. The stores were jammed. Narcisse loaded the car with all the canned meat and vegetables they would sell him, till the springs rode

down to the axles, and stowed it aboard the *Angélique*. Then
he went back for another load, but by that time all the
canned food was gone. He bought flour and beans, which no
one had thought of yet. He transported these supplies alone,
trusting no one, and was very tired when he got them all
aboard. He was reluctant to leave the *Angélique*, but there
was little activity on the waterfront. The boat owners, he
supposed, had more confidence in their ability to escape than
most people. He went home, pondering, I've got a lot of
food, but it won't keep a family of twelve very long.

"Put everything but breakfast into the car," he told Angélique.

"Everything?"

"No, dear; just anything we can eat, anything the kids
need to keep warm, blankets, shoes, coats. Grand dieu, Angélique, *you* know what they need."

"It won't all fit in the car," she said, biting her lip.

"Then we'll make several trips during the night, you
and I."

"Leave the children alone?"

"Angélique, nobody's going to steal *people*. That's the last
thing they'll steal. Useless mouths."

It was growing dark. She began loading the car. "Don't
turn on the lights," he said.

"Where are you going?"

"I'm going to see Archange."

In the rectory Archange was seated behind his desk in his
study, while frightened people came and went. For all of
them he had the same word: a big ship would arrive at Percé
tomorrow. He had it from Madame Boucher at the station.
There was nothing to worry about. The ship could accommodate the entire population of the village. All who wished

to go could go. But no, he could give them no assurance that
the weather would return to normal. One could hope but one
could not be sure. Everyone must do as he saw fit. And no, it
was unlikely that the little old lady could take her cat.
"Leave it here, madame. Many of us do not plan to evacuate."

"Aren't you going, Father?"

"Of course not." He was white and drawn and he looked
at her sternly.

"I won't go either then. I certainly couldn't leave Marianne
behind."

He nodded and smiled as she left.

Narcisse waited till they were all gone.

"Well, Narcisse?" said Archange.

"You know why I've come, Archange."

"I suspect, but you've already heard my answer."

"I'm leaving the minute I can buy some more diesel oil.
You must come with me."

The curé looked at his brother, who read his wry expression.

"But you *must!*" Narcisse said.

Archange laughed softly. "I'm so glad you came! I haven't
laughed all day. Narcisse, you do me good, you strengthen
me. The others, they drain me. I am so very tired. But you
are a tower of strength. Utterly predictable in a very mad
world." He poured a single glass of wine and set it before
Narcisse.

"None for yourself?" Narcisse said.

"Confessions in an hour." The curé shrugged. "Everybody
thinks he's monstrously wicked tonight. They aren't, of
course. Some of them actually blame themselves for the
cold, poor things."

"I've decided to sail tomorrow before there's a real panic, and I beg you to come with me," Narcisse said, pleading.

"I thought you would," said Archange, "and I wholly approve. I've got a couple of drums of oil in the garage. You'll be needing that."

"How did you know?"

"Well, won't you? The boats are buying it up on the sly and there isn't much left. But I got you a couple of drums."

"I'll get it tonight," said Narcisse.

"Good."

They looked at each other.

"You're sure you won't come?"

"I didn't lie when I told the people a big ship will put in tomorrow and evacuate the whole village. Others will come later for those who gather from the farms in the interior. I'll wait around a while, Narcisse."

"You actually believe the ship will come?"

"I do not totally disbelieve it. And if it does not, there'll be another soon. There were hundreds of ships in the St. Lawrence. One will have a compassionate captain. They've dumped their cargoes and they're under orders to evacuate everybody all down the coast. One will not turn a deaf ear. The authorities are handling things very efficiently and the radio says there is very little panic."

"On *my* radio Madame Boucher couldn't raise a single ship."

"I know. She became a little hysterical, I'm afraid. They shut her down. Later she got an official answer about the evacuation ship."

"And you really think it will come?"

Archange shrugged his shoulders and exposed his palms in an eloquent Gallic gesture and smiled. "That or another."

"I'll see you when I come back for the oil," Narcisse said. "Maybe you'll have changed your mind."

"Judas did," Archange said, chuckling.

Narcisse and Angélique took three loads of food and supplies to the boat. It was three o'clock in the morning when, dead tired, Narcisse went back to the rectory to get the oil. The curé was still hearing confessions and Narcisse could not see him that night. The *Angélique* now had three tankfuls of fuel, one in the tank and two in spare drums. Narcisse was not satisfied. There was a long way to go and many mouths to feed. But he could do no more; he fell into bed with his clothes on and slept deeply till the dawn awakened him with a sense of impending doom. He thought Angélique beside him was dead, so motionless did she sleep. Then he saw her breathing and smiled.

"Pauvre petite," he said. "I've been having nightmares."

"Ouf!" she said, as he kissed her. "What time is it?"

"Time to get up and go."

"Well, we'll have to have breakfast first," she said.

He looked out of the window: no bells, no sirens, no whistles, no crowds. It seemed a very normal morning, save for the continuing snow.

"All right," he said.

When they had finished she said, "I've always wanted to have a meal and simply throw the dishes out."

"Why don't you? There's plenty of pots and pans and stuff on the boat."

"No, we might be coming back and I'd want to have things neat."

So the children helped with the dishes as usual.

Narcisse was not satisfied with the food supply. He went to the warehouse of the *Pêcheurs-Unis* and loaded the car with packing crates of salt cod. It was concentrated, it would sustain life; he had made five trips when the guard approached and stopped him.

"Hello, Narcisse."

"Hello, Jean Paul."

"Taking a little stuff?"

"As you see."

"So am I," said Jean Paul, the guard. "I'm leaving too." He winked and disappeared, leaving the warehouse unguarded. Shortly Narcisse heard his old truck roaring away.

Jean Paul trusts the appearance of the evacuation ship no more than I do, thought Narcisse.

There was subdued activity around the waterfront now. All the fishermen knew each other, but they spoke very little, exchanged embarrassed nods, and each man went about his business. Narcisse noted a great many crates and packing boxes being loaded aboard the various craft. Fishermen are forehanded, he thought grimly.

It was time to go now. He drove the car up to the house. The still-blooming roses were bending over with snow. Archange was in the living room.

"I thought you might need somebody to drive the car back after you leave," he said. His face was pale as a ghost.

"Archange," Narcisse whispered. *"That ship isn't coming!"*

"Oh yes it is. But it's full. We're promised another. Can you take an extra passenger, Narcisse?"

"Thank God! Of course I can."

"That little old woman who wouldn't leave her cat. I was wondering if you could make room for her."

Narcisse wept. "No."

"Oh, very well," said Archange. "There'll be another ship soon. Now let's get this brood of yours into the car. It'll make quite a load, I should think."

"I'll have to make two trips."

"I shouldn't advise it," the curé said. "I'd have brought my own car but I'm afraid it was stolen during the night."

"Are things that bad?"

"They're not getting any better. When the people found out that the evacuation ship was full they naturally became nervous."

"Then it's one trip," Narcisse said grimly.

Thirteen bodies crammed into the car. The curé said, "A little salt between the layers and you'd have a full load, Narcisse," but Narcisse could think of no answer in the same spirit of levity and was silent. From the wharf they trooped onto the *Angélique*, Angélique carrying the baby, the bigger children helping the smaller ones.

Archange grinned. "Au revoir, Father Noah!"

"Come aboard!" shouted Narcisse.

"I'll catch the next boat."

Narcisse started down the gangplank to get him, but paused. A group were gathering on the wharf. They had suitcases and duffle bags and frightened faces, and en masse they presented the appearance of a mob, though he knew every face and they were old friends.

"I can't take you all," Narcisse cried, "so I take no one except Archange."

"We're promised a ship tomorrow," the curé said, calming them.

"Come aboard, Archange!"

"Next trip, Narcisse."

With his own hands, while no one dared stop him, Archange cast off the *Angélique's* mooring lines.

"You'd better go now, Narcisse," he said to his brother.

A gap of water widened between the boat and the wharf as the *Angélique* slowly drifted away. "You imbecile!" Narcisse cried angrily. "Very well. Go to blazes!"

"I rather think it will be to the contrary," the curé said, smiling thinly.

"Narcisse, that ship isn't coming!" Angélique said in horror.

The curé heard her. "Don't say that!" he cried. "Of course it's coming. You'll frighten the people. Come now, mes enfants," he addressed them, "it's coming all right. I, your curé, I tell you it's coming."

"Don't cause a panic," Narcisse warned her. "Maybe it's really coming."

"I'm sorry," she said.

Narcisse started the motor. Angélique and the children lined the rail and waved good-bye to their lifelong neighbors.

Black-robed and smiling ironically Archange stood before the crowd and blessed Narcisse as he pulled away. "Adieu, Brother Noah. You pilot a precious cargo. One of your girls may surprise you. May you find your Ararat."

The crowd now hurried away. As the distance grew Narcisse saw the black-robed figure, now white with snow on the shoulders and the broad-brimmed clerical hat, one hand still raised in a wave of farewell. Then the hand traced a cross, and the figure got into Narcisse's car.

Narcisse called the Percé station. "Madame Boucher! Madame Boucher!"

She came in at once. "I'm not supposed to be on. Quickly, Narcisse."

"Is the evacuation ship really coming tomorrow? Archange said it was."

The destroyer cut in, "Percé, shut down!"

There was a moment of dead air, then Madame Boucher came back. "He's trying to get everybody on the other fishing boats."

"Percé, shut down."

"What are you going to do?" Narcisse asked.

There was no answer.

The children asked, "Where are we going?"

It struck him that he did not know.

"South," he said.

CHAPTER 10

He set a course due south with a strong wind directly astern, which increased his speed, as did a slow new current that never before had streamed out of the polar sea. It continued to snow, every day the same light unceasing downfall. Visibility was poor. The following seas were leaden, wide spaced from crest to crest, and ugly, like the big slow swells that beat upon a shore and advise the informed weather watcher that a storm is raging somewhere near and soon will strike. Narcisse waited for it, but it did not come: just the steady wind with an arctic chill in it, the high seas and the snowfall that never stopped. It was depressing weather and the children, whom he kept inside, complained and argued among themselves, asking why they could not play on the deck as they always had before when Papa took them for an outing.

Angélique made them holiday meals every day. "The fresh meat will spoil if we don't eat it up," she said. "We could crate it up and let it freeze on the deck, though, couldn't we?"

Narcisse shook his head. It was too cold for comfort but

not cold enough to preserve fresh meat. "Better eat it up, I think." He reproached himself that he had not thought to bring a bag of salt. He could have salted it down like cod. But he had no empty hogsheads either. Every container aboard was chock full of supplies. "Let them enjoy it while they can. Soon enough we'll be on survival rations." But thank God there was plenty of those. Only the perishables, the delicacies, would be lacking.

Although there was plenty of food the problem of water might soon become serious. "I wish you had a distiller aboard," Angélique said.

"We've never been out as long as this. No fishing boats have them."

"How long will we be out?"

"Till the weather clears and it gets warmer. It's bound to be warmer down south."

The course due south took him out of the Gulf of St. Lawrence. Then he turned west, hoping to water at Halifax. But a radio had been set up at Halifax, which had been hit, and appeals were going out in English and French for ships to come in and pick up refugees. They were promising payment in cash, supplies or jewels.

"Jewels?" said Angélique. "It must be very bad."

"They'd swarm aboard and swamp us," Narcisse said. "No Halifax for me."

"The poor things," Angélique said.

Narcisse swore.

He conserved his fuel, jealous of every drop, watching the gauge and scowling at it as if scowling would reverse its downward trend. Then, the wind holding and no storm coming out of the north, he stopped the motor and ran up the sail. The *Angélique* was a cranky sailer with her one canvas and low freeboard. But he did not know how far south he would have to go till the freak weather cleared.

The deck was three inches deep in snow. One day, to clean it off, he started the motor and sluiced it down with sea water.

"The footing's firmer now," he said. "Better take the bigger kids up for some fresh air." It had grown stuffy below deck, clammy and cold, since without the motor there was no heat.

They loved the exercise, and their cheeks looked healthy and pink again when they returned, and they had a hearty appetite for supper that night, which Angélique prepared over the oil stove in the galley.

"Narcisse?" she said seriously, when they were tucked away for the night.

"Yes?"

"Narcisse, I think it's safer below. I don't think we'd better take an airing again till we get farther south."

"Why?"

One of the children, she said, had slipped and fallen, sliding dangerously close to the rail.

"Grand dieu! I didn't see it."

"We were aft, watching the waves astern. They fascinate the children. They look so high you think they're going to curl right over the stern."

"You know they never do. They just lift us up and roll right under us."

"Yes, but it was a great game for the children. I wanted to teach them. But the snow keeps falling even after you've hosed it all overboard, and I'm afraid of an accident."

"I'll run a net all around the rail," Narcisse said. "Then nobody can fall overboard."

"Narcisse?"

"What else?" he said, grinning.

"I don't know whether it happened by accident, but Angélique did something today that gave me an idea about the water."

"Did you take her out too?"

"Just for a moment. She looked *so* pale and frail, Narcisse."

"Dammit, you might have slipped and both of you would have fallen overboard."

"Well, we didn't."

"Now I damn well sure will put up that net. I couldn't fish with it without a crew anyhow. I'll make the damnedest strongest rail any boat ever had."

"As I was holding Angélique she lifted up her little head and opened her mouth and ate the snowflakes—that is, she didn't really eat, of course, but she let them fall into her mouth and ran her tongue over her lips and smiled as if she liked the taste. That's what gave me the idea about the water."

Narcisse grinned. "She was probably only yawning, but I'm grateful for the idea. Some little teacher, eh, that one? I will personally award her a diploma. Why didn't I think of that?"

"It's all right to melt the snow and use it for drinking water, isn't it?"

Narcisse pondered. "It was all right in Percé. I don't know how it is here."

"It isn't red any more."

"I'll catch some and save it for an emergency. Well, dieu bénisse that little Angélique, even if she was only yawning. But I'm going to put in to shore the first chance I get and fill up our water tanks. It ought to clear up by Boston."

He rigged the net, double thickness, from deck to rail, and scooped up a quantity of pure white snow next day,

taking only the top layer and avoiding scraping the deck
with his shovel, since the deck would be salty with sea
water. Then he sluiced down the decks again and headed
more to the west towards Boston.

With the wind on her quarter the *Angélique* wallowed and
pitched. Narcisse would be glad when they reached the
Boston wharves.

There were no Boston wharves. Boston too had been hit.
The snow was still falling. He came very close in shore,
thinking he had missed the channel. Suddenly, out of the
mist, he heard frantic voices, and shortly, like ghosts, appeared scores of rowboats and pleasure craft, bearing down
upon him like an enemy fleet. He could not understand their
English, but the note of desperation in their voices was un-
mistakable.

"They've spotted me," he told Angélique. "They've only
got little boats. I'm bigger than they are. They'll swarm
aboard if I let them, the pirates!"

He turned the *Angélique* about and started the motor.

"Take the tiller, Angélique. Steer out to sea."

He sat on the taffrail with the rifle in his hand. He left
the sailboats and week-end motorboats behind. But one
cabin cruiser was faster than the *Angélique*. It was a gas-
powered craft with high speed but a restricted range.

"No, you don't!" Narcisse said.

He shot at it as it neared, aiming carefully at the man at
the helm. The craft suddenly lost control and veered crazily
away. From a loud speaker came a voice, "God damn you!
God damn you to hell!"

Even a Gaspésian knew the common English expression
"goddam." Narcisse smiled grimly. If I wouldn't take my
neighbors I won't take strangers, he thought.

Angélique at the tiller said, "Narcisse, did you kill a man?"

"I only fired into the air to scare him off."

"Maybe he was coming out to help us."

"I don't think anybody is helping anybody any more. It's every man for himself."

All over the world similar scenes of self-preservation were enacted. Most are unknown. Some must have been actions of devotion, like Archange's, that would serve for canonization. Some are known to have been so hideous that they do not bear the telling, for sheer animal ferocity. Between the brute's and the martyr's response to the peril of The Big Ice lay this action of Narcisse Bolduc with his family: rather average, when not pushed; self-preserving when pushed too far; but totally normal. He and Angélique belonged to the same broad mass of unspectacular humanity as Bill and Betty Young. Narcisse acted swiftly, without conscious cerebration, when instinct warned him that survival was at stake.

From the Gaspé to Boston the slow persistent snow had fallen without letup. Narcisse judged that conditions ashore must be similar, and he decided to avoid the coast till the weather cleared. If the Bostonians were desperately anxious to migrate, how much more desperate would be the survivors of New York City, with its millions of starving people, he thought.

He did not know this part of the American coast but he assumed that enough would be left of New York to recognize. Surely some of that mighty pile of concrete and steel would still be there. Then he would establish his position for sure. He had not been able to see the stars or shoot the sun since leaving home, and he was uncertain of his latitude.

In the latitude where he guessed Manhattan Island ought to be there was nothing but a half-submerged reef. He avoided the reef and steered south, the north wind strong on his stern.

"That might have been New York," he thought. "New York would have attracted a vast concentration of missiles." For several days he twisted the dials of the radio. He could hear voices and code very far away, but nothing close. He had entered an area of total local radio silence. He studied his charts in perplexity, and ran his finger over the long string of towns that constituted the North American seaboard: Boston, New York, Philadelphia, names he knew as markets for the fish of the *Pêcheurs-Unis*—an enormous metropolitan population here. Washington was close by; he knew that had been hit. Wilmington, where they built the ships and where there were big chemical works named after a Frenchman, he knew would have been a prime target. Probably all the cities were destroyed. That would account for the radio silence. It would be unwise to go ashore. The enormity of the catastrophe was borne in upon him, and the terrifying danger posed by the survivors. He thought of Archange's last words and wondered whether Noah ever had worried about supplies in the Ark. But Noah had a commission from God and Narcisse Bolduc did not. Still, except for miracles, the business of feeding all those animals must have been difficult, and the sanitary conditions must have been terrible.

"You'd better do the laundry in sea water from now on," he told Angélique. "We've lots of salt-water soap."

"It'll chafe the baby, Narcisse. You can't wash diapers in sea water."

"Then use the water we get by melting the snow. I want to keep the rest for drinking."

He did not know when he would be able to go ashore and refill the casks from some pure water or creek. Maybe he would be lucky enough to find a farm with a well near the shore. But maybe the American farmers all have running water, he mused. He wished he were traveled and educated. How little he really knew. How little anybody knew.

Food was no problem, though by now all the fresh meat and vegetables were gone and the children had begun to complain of the monotony of the canned food, much of which they had to eat cold. Narcisse was saving oil and navigating by sail. The north wind still held steady but seemed to be losing some of its force. One day he said, "Angélique, I think we're getting out of the worst of it."

"We must be halfway to the equator," she said wearily. "It seems so long." She looked wan and tired. In addition to all her housekeeping she had to relieve him at the wheel since, patently, he could not stay awake twenty-four hours a day.

Then the snow changed pinkish again, and it began to rain. It alarmed him at first, then he said, "Well, this is how it started; maybe this is how it will stop. Tomorrow I'll catch a fish. It smells like good fishing weather." He wondered what his position was, but the sea looked good, felt good and smelled clean and clear. That day the sun came out. The deck dried and the pale children romped in the sunlight. Narcisse fished for ten minutes and brought in three fat Gaspésian cod.

"I told you I smelled good fishing," he said, grinning. "Now we'll have a feast. Fry the livers, Angélique. The kids look as if they could use the vitamins. Have we got any onions left?"

"I've saved a few in case of colds."

"Good. Just like home!"

"Where are we, Narcisse?" she asked.

He paused, remembering the tarpon.

"We are off the coast of South Carolina," he said soberly.

There ought not to be Gaspésian cod off the coast of South Carolina. "We'll hit Charleston soon."

But where Charleston ought to have been there was only a large indentation in the coastline, no trace of a city.

"I guess there aren't any big cities anywhere in the world," he said.

In this area also he did not dare land.

With the cessation of rain and snow he began again to worry about the water supply, though they feasted merrily on the cod.

"Narcisse, Angélique loved the cod liver. I mashed it up, and she loved it."

"Onions, too?" Narcisse said, grinning.

"Well, I put a little in."

"Couldn't hurt her. Do her good. She was pretty pale."

"Narcisse, now she won't nurse."

"What?"

"She won't nurse at all. So I gave her solid food. I puréed it, of course. She absolutely gobbled it up." Angélique looked dejected. "None of the others ever weaned themselves. I had to wean them."

"I suppose they're all different each time," Narcisse said, thinking about the dwindling water supply.

"Well, I don't like it. It isn't natural."

South of Charleston, Narcisse came across a large river. There was no name for it on his charts, but he entered the estuary, steering clear of the banks, which were marshy and low, keeping a sharp lookout for boats that might be hostile and cut off his retreat to the open sea. He was looking for a fresh-water creek.

He saw no boats and the cat tails and marine vegetation that grew near the shore were scorched. The missile that had destroyed Charleston had apparently obliterated all life for many miles around. Or perhaps more than one had fallen. He wished he had a Geiger Counter aboard in this desolate area. He knew there had been no radioactive fallout from any of the other missiles, but the burnt-out landscape was so depressing to contemplate and the whole world had been so fearful of fallout ever since Hiroshima that a Geiger Counter would have given him confidence. But a Gaspésian trawler did not include such an instrument among its gear. You've got to have faith in something and not expect perpetual confirmation of everything, he thought, and relied on the analysis of the red rain that his brother had given him, and pressed forward on his course upriver. There were bound to be tributaries. One would be fresh and clear, and he would anchor and replenish his water.

The river forked, and he purposely took the smaller stream with the swifter current. He had lowered the sail and was under power now. The parched terrain seemed to have been farmland, for there were dead cattle in the fields, but no dwellings or people. He dropped a bucket and tested the water. It tasted all right, but he feared contamination, typhus, from the decaying livestock; and proceeded farther upstream till the current became so swift that the *Angélique* made very slow headway against it. He was jealous of every drop of diesel oil, and yet humans cannot drink diesel oil. He balanced his needs. Water was winning.

At length in a blackened area where he saw no trace of death he anchored and made his decision. The narrow river ran swift and clear. It tasted good. It took him three hours to fill the empty casks with his bucket, filtering it through a cheesecloth. There were healthy minnows in it and some crawfish. "Well, they're alive," he thought, "so the water's OK." It was refreshing to drink after the stale supply on the

Angélique. The children drank it and smacked their lips. Narcisse turned downstream again, satisfied.

But when Angélique held a cup of the water to the baby, the baby began to cry and shook her head violently from side to side, as infants do when something unpalatable is offered them. By chance or design little Angélique knocked the cup out of her mother's hand and said, "No!"

"Narcisse," said Angélique, "could something be wrong with that river water?"

"I don't think so," he said. "It tasted all right. I suppose we'll know in a day or two if we all get diarrhoea; and if we do we'll eat a lot of cheese. There wasn't anything dead around, but river water sometimes has bugs in it."

"The baby wouldn't drink it."

"Well, don't force her. Maybe she's a good Gaspésian and likes well water even if it is stale."

"Narcisse, the baby spoke! She said 'No,' and knocked the cup out of my hand."

"That's impossible," he said.

But that night, as he thought it over, he dumped overboard all the river water and cleaned the casks with soda and rinsed them with fresh water and set them out to dry in the sun. Then he scraped them down to the wood. He was intensely frightened and looked for signs of diarrhoea or even a stomach upset. None occurred. Meanwhile he had no more water than he had had before he went up the river, indeed less, since the family were consuming it very day and he had used some to flush the casks. It was absolutely essential to refill them, and, a day's sail farther south, he steered inshore again and ran up another river.

There, in a similar desolate but less painfully burned spot he refilled his casks, this time from a well by a deserted farmhouse. The frame building seemed only to have been scorched. A frightfully burned old Negro couple lay dead in their beds in the shack, their hair singed. The wife, who was very fat, had apparently succumbed as she was trying to bandage the husband, who was very thin. In the ruins of the barn a mule had cooked, and a milk cow lay bloated and crawling with maggots, but Narcisse thought that the well, located on a rise behind the outbuildings, had probably not been contaminated. That was how they dug wells on the Gaspé, away from the seepage of the farm. There were scrawny chickens in the remains of the chicken house, cackling, scratching, uncared for and hungry. Some had singed feathers. Narcisse looped a string around their feet and took a backload of them aboard the *Angélique* and, on further reflection, went back for some sacks of chicken feed. "Since you haven't died yet," he addressed them, "you must be pretty healthy and you'll keep the family Bolduc alive." They were certainly no good to their dead owners any more. He fashioned a chicken coop of fishing nets on the *Angélique's* deck and every day the children fed them. They began to thrive with renewed good food and attention.

"Those which are not roosters will lay eggs," Narcisse instructed his family, who laughed. They already knew that. "And we can have omelettes."

Little Angélique drank the well water without protest. Then her mother cooked the chickens and made a thick purée for the child who would not nurse. Little Angélique chewed it thoughtfully with her four front teeth, burped nicely and snored off to sleep, perfectly happy.

"She looks so old," Angélique said to Narcisse. Lately she had taken to talking in whispers in the baby's hearing, as if the baby would understand. "Narcisse, I'd swear she said 'No' to that water."

"No baby says yes or no or anything else for a year!" Narcisse said angrily. "You only imagined it." He scowled as he always did when he was troubled by something he did not understand. He left the cabin. He did not want her to remind him that he had dumped the water overboard and scraped the casks. He did not want to be reminded that he agreed that the bébé looked far too old. He had heard stories of freak children who had grown wrinkled and old and died of old age at the age of seven, their bodies bent and their hair white. Nine times the good Lord had given him normal healthy children. Why should the good Lord give him a freak for the tenth? What had he done?

The north wind still blew, but with less force, and Narcisse was compelled to use the engine more, and the oil level began to drop on the gauge. He was off the coast of Georgia now. It was low, flat and full of small inlets, beside which stood untouched towns. He could see water tanks and buildings. More ships had begun to make their appearance, too, all heading south. Through his glass he saw launches heading out for one that was anchored. There seemed to be a great number of them, scurrying around the vessel like ants around a crust of bread. He saw a winch hoist a stretcher aboard and there was the white of bandages.

"Evacuating," he muttered, and steered away.

In the latitude of Jacksonville, Florida, which showed as a large town on his chart, on an estuary that connected with a large inland lake, the thought occurred to him, "Maybe I am at the end of my voyage. Maybe here I can get work." There had been no snow for many days. He deemed himself south of the queer cruel cold that had smitten the higher latitudes. Here, perhaps, he could rest and make a home for his family.

In view of all he had seen, the obvious desperation of multitudes to migrate, he did not aim as high as a cottage ashore;

people would be hungry; people would steal, especialy from a foreigner who could not speak their language. But he could turn that universal hunger to his benefit; he was still a good fisherman, and had his card as the head of the *Pêcheurs-Unis* to prove it. He would be in demand. He would get a good job from the Jacksonville authorities: and one way or another he could keep the family aboard till things got more settled and he learned more about what had happened.

In a hopeful mood he steered towards the mouth of the St. Johns River, but where Jacksonville had stood, with its skyscrapers, airports, concrete causeways and multi-wharved waterfront, all was now gone, volatilized like all the other great American cities, and the estuary of the St. Johns River had been widened by twenty miles.

"I should have known," Narcisse muttered. "All the big places are gone."

There was no answer but to press ever southward, conserving now both oil and water, since the sail was of little help and he did not know how far he would have to go. Perhaps all the way to Panama and beyond. The thought of the seven-hundred-mile stretch of open ocean between North and South America was so fantastic, so contrary to every stable fact he ever had learned, so heretically at variance with any map ever drawn, that he scarcely could think about it. And South America, if South America was to be his goal, was as distant and alien as the moon. He kept close to shore, hoping to sight a happy place. When things get very bad, it is normal to hope for abnormal release. In this most abnormal phase of planetary history it came for Narcisse Bolduc.

Angélique went up to the pilot house and said to him, "Narcisse, the radio's speaking in French."

"It is?"

"It's coming from New Orleans. New Orleans was hit too, but they've set up a stand-by station, and they're recruiting workers."

"Workers for what?"

"They're building refugee cities all down the Florida coast and along the coast of the Gulf of Mexico. Anybody who can use a hammer or saw can get a job. They're building these cities to take in all the displaced persons from the north. They're coming down by the millions."

"I'll try the next likely port," he said dubiously. Narcisse had seen thousands of refugees in Korea during that war, and had not trusted them. Even less did he trust refugees by the millions; they became more predatory than fish, than the worst of fish, sharks. He looked at the half-dozen little Bolducs playing on the deck. He looked at his wife, Angé-lique. She was thinner with worry and work. He looked at his boat, not so neat as she had been but staunch, safe and dependable. He oiled his rifle and steered towards a wharf on the shore that had a big sign, "Help Wanted."

The sign was amateurishly scrawled, but an attempt had been made to dress it up and make it festive and inviting by stringing some plastic pennants that had been rifled from a deserted garage or supermarket.

Angélique said, "They want help, poor things. I know the English words. I don't know how we can help."

Narcisse said, "No, that is how les anglais advertise jobs in the papers for people who want work. It probably has something to do with the broadcast you heard from New Orleans. They're probably building a refugee city here."

It did not look much like a city. The harbor was deserted; the *Angélique* was the only boat. Yet there were many wharves, and once it must have been a popular Florida re-sort. A number of men in leather jackets were idling on the wharf, calling over the water to the *Angélique,* motioning with their arms to come alongside. No one was fishing.

"Maybe there's plenty of food here and they don't have to fish," Narcisse said, "but I don't like the looks of this place."

He swept the waterfront with his glasses. Boathouses were open and empty, the doors and windows smashed. Shops bore similar traces of violence.

"There's been looting here," Narcisse said. "There aren't any women or children around; that's not normal. Get the family below, Angélique. I'm going in a bit and try to talk to them."

He did not stop the motor and kept his hand on the reverse for a quick retreat. Angélique shepherded the children below and peeked through the curtains of a porthole. The men on the wharf continued to motion the *Angélique* in. Narcisse was close now but wary, and he kept about twenty feet away from the wharf. They shouted to him in English. He shouted questions in French: What was this place? Was there work? Was there safe habitation? Was there plenty of food and water?

He could see them clearly now. Their clothes were new and ill-fitting. Most were unshaven and several were drunk. A man who seemed to be their leader held out a fistful of bills, pointed to the *Angélique* covetously, made a pantomime of giving the bills to Narcisse.

"No, thank you, m'sieur," said Narcisse with a curse, and gunned the motor into a furious reverse.

On his ears fell a chorus of "goddams" and the men on the wharf shook their fists as the *Angélique* curved out in a creamy white wake towards open water.

Angélique came into the pilot house.

"What were they?"

"God knows. Escaped prisoners or lunatics or both. The

'Help Wanted' sign was a trap. They wanted to steal the boat. They're probably the last ones left after the rest were evacuated."

A bullet whistled overhead and a hole appeared in the exhaust stack. Narcisse pushed Angélique down behind the protection of the bulkhead. "Duck!"

He was tempted to fire back, but they had no boats to follow and it did not seem worth while.

"If one, if only one had pointed to the shore, I'd have trusted them. But not one did. They weren't thinking about the shore. There's nothing there. They only wanted to get away."

"Where shall we go now, Narcisse?"

"South."

Always south.

CHAPTER 11

THAT evening, in the spectacular sunset that made the sea look like fresh blood, he came across a derelict private yacht. It presented a most unnerving aspect. All the upper woodwork was burned away; all the metal above a sharply defined line four feet from the waterline was gone. The glass ports had fused and hung in drops like grotesquely magnified tears. But below the line of obliteration all was as it had been before. The yacht looked as if a razor-sharp flame had sheared off its upper works. It looked like a picture the top of which some mischievous child had snipped off with shears.

Narcisse drew alongside and clambered aboard the hulk. There should be fresh water in the tanks below. He wanted nothing more. In the crimson light of the sunset, illuminating the interior of the hold through gaps in the deck above, Narcisse beheld with admiration one of the most beautiful engine rooms he had ever seen. The yacht must have belonged to some millionaire. The chrome and brass shone like silver and gold and the steel catwalks were immaculately clean. There was the good sailor smell of fresh oiled surfaces. It was neat as a Navy ship and the compact turbine was painted robin's egg blue. But nothing beside remained but the hull, like a foundation without a building. All that had lived, owned and directed on the upper works was gone with the blast that had melted the ports into teardrops. Yet not quite all. He came upon the body of a man, whose head had been savagely battered with a hammer. Nearby lay an officer's cap, stained with blood and brains, with a gold braid over the vizor. It was probably the chief engineer. Someone had killed him after the blast, making off with the life raft or life jacket that would not accommodate them both and for which they had fought for possession.

There was plenty of water. There was also more fuel oil than the *Angélique* had tanks for, but it felt heavier than diesel oil and Narcisse did not dare mix it with his dwindling supply for fear the motor would never start again.

That night he transported case after case of gourmet food from the hulk to the *Angélique*. The provisions reflected a millionaire's taste and extravagance. The yacht had been stocked for a pleasure cruise and a banquet every night. The children could eat caviar now if they liked.

His conscience smote him. "If I'd known I would find so much food I could have taken a lot of neighbors with me," he said, "and Archange would have come."

"I'm sure they got out," Angélique said, stowing away the food with the older children's help. "There were lots of other boats like ours."

Narcisse hoped so.

"There are cases and cases of champagne," he said. "I wish they were water."

The problem of transferring the water from the fresh-water tanks of the derelict to the *Angélique* was very real.

"I could do it with the bucket of course," he said. "I will if I have to, but it will take two or three days."

"I expect it's worth it," she said.

"I'll sleep on it."

It was an engineering problem. He would tackle it tomorrow. It was dark now and he was dead tired. The children were asleep, all but the baby, and the *Angélique* and the derelict rode side by side in the calm with a single line holding them together.

"There's not a trace of wind any more," he said, frowning. Fuel oil was going to be another problem.

"I brought you a bottle of wine," he said. He and Angélique did not know much about champagne, but he had found a wine cellar aboard the hulk that would have served as a pilot plant for a first-class hotel. "It isn't Gaspésian, but it's delicious."

She saw he was troubled and trying to hide it from her. "We'll celebrate tonight," she said. "We could take the hulk in tow if we had to."

"Yes, I've considered that. We can trail our own larder behind."

"Of course we can."

But they both knew you couldn't do that in anything but a dead calm.

"Narcisse, there's nobody alive over there, is there?"

"No, dear, nobody."

"There wasn't when you found it, was there?"

"On my honor, no!"

"I know what you'd have done if there had been."

"Yes, if he'd been hostile."

"I guess everybody feels the same way now. It's awful, but I'm getting used to it. There's nobody to enforce the laws and everybody makes his own laws. I suppose it's natural to look after yourself and your family first, no matter who else suffers."

"There's been plenty of that," he said soberly.

"Probably savages felt like that before there were nations: the warrior, the family, the tribe. That's as far as they could think when there weren't so many people."

"There aren't so many any more, and they're pretty savage," he said, yawning.

"I'll listen to New Orleans while you sleep." She drew a blanket over him and kissed his forehead as he dropped off, half frowning, still puzzling over the problem of transferring the water from the hulk to the tanks of the *Angélique*.

She watched him a while till his forehead smoothed, then listened to the New Orleans broadcast, keeping the volume low so as not to awaken him. What she heard made her glad that Narcisse's instinct had kept him away from that part of the Florida coast. They had chanced upon one of the many places that could not be policed, from which every decent citizen had fled and where land pirates had set up an unholy municipality. Not since the pirate empires of Madagascar and the Spanish Main had there flourished such centers of unbridled abandon and crime, and it was unpunishable because no one could be spared from the greater work, which the New Orleans radio also described. She would tell him about it in the morning; it promised security and safety; but not tonight, since he was sleeping too peacefully after his exhausting labor.

During the night the *Angélique* nudged against the hulk a couple of times, and Angélique trembled. It is very dangerous for two loosely tied craft to drift close together even in the calmest of seas, and this sea was. Even in such circumstances an unexpected gust of wind could send them crash-

ing together, and who knew whether there might not be
a gust of wind in a planetary disruption of weather?

At dawn Narcisse awakened and leapt from his bunk,
grinning. "I think I know a way to *pump* fresh water on
board!" he shouted to Angélique as a good morning greeting.
"I dreamed I was sitting on my big fat—"

"Narcisse! The children!"

"—lazybones, squirting a hose into a tank, into the casks,
everywhere, and I didn't stir a muscle!"

"But the hulk is without power."

"Power is all she lacks and we've got it. The generator
will do the job. Now, now, Angélique, we have everything!"

Till she saw his exultation she had not realized how worried he had been. She had thought she was the only one.
It was like him to have hidden his fears. She did not credit
herself with the fact that it was like her too.

Narcisse clambered aboard the hulk and disappeared below. Quicker than he had been with the cases of food he
reappeared again with an end of fire hose, which he coiled
on the deck. Angélique noted he was still smiling broadly.
His hands were begrimed with oil and dirt but there was
triumph in his face.

"Throw me the work lamp," he called. It was an electric
bulb with a protective wire cage on a long well-insulated
cord that plugged into a generator outlet. The boats were
closely tied. She practically handed it to him. He disappeared below again.

He removed the bulb and cage and bared the wires and
attached them to the terminals of the hulk's fresh-water
pump, crossing his fingers. It was an American yacht, not
one of those crazy 220-volt foreign ones of les anglais.

He returned to the *Angélique* dragging the fire hose behind him. "Now we will see if I get water or if I burn out

the generator. She was a pretty big pump I'm trying to energize, pretty big." His face was tense and sober now.

He started the motor and watched the meter on the generator. It shot up alarmingly high and he knew he was overloading it. But water poured merrily out of the hose; he needed the water more than the generator. He rushed to the deck and directed the precious stream into a cask, then another, then more, till they were all full. He was about to fill the *Angélique's* fresh-water tank next, but suddenly the cord that supplied the power began to melt, then burst into flame.

"Shut it off! Shut the motor off!" he shouted to Angélique. Angélique had already done so. She had seen the smoke and recognized the danger.

But he shook his head. The cord was still burning in spots. "The cord's ruined," he said.

"Maybe there's another on the hulk."

"There is. I saw several. But I'm afraid to try again. I'm afraid for the generator now."

Till noon he transferred more fresh water, bucket by bucket, by hand, into the *Angélique's* tank, till it was half full. On a fishing trip, that would suffice his small crew for a week. For ten children, plus himself and Angélique, it might last five days with rationing. The supply in the casks would last another five. Ten days was not long, but it was longer than anyone in Panama had had.

He would willingly have transferred diesel oil, if necessary by the teacupful, but there was none in the hulk, only the heavy fuel oil suitable for a steam turbine, and he was not enough of an engineer to know whether a diesel would run on it and he dared not mix it with his scant remaining supply. Hundreds of gallons of precious fuel ten feet away, and alcohol to have thinned it. I don't know how, and I can't take a chance, he thought, as he left it.

"Have we water enough to last to New Orleans?" Angélique asked him.

"Yes, I think so, with care. Why?"

She told him about the New Orleans broadcast. "Most places aren't safe, but New Orleans still is. It's some sort of a recruitment center. They're rebuilding The Dam. That's the name it's got now: the whole Isthmus of Panama. They say it's the only way to make the weather normal again. It's complicated; I didn't understand it all, but they'll explain it every day. All nations are helping. All nations are threatened with death by freezing if they don't. The war is over. Workers are needed, thousands and thousands and thousands. Millions if they can get them. Especially workers with boats. But you don't have to have a boat. They'll supply passage from New Orleans for anybody able and willing to work. I don't know what happens to old people and orphans and people in hospitals."

"What about a man with ten children?"

"Narcisse, I've seen you break your back all day for those ten children."

"You do the same thing."

"They must know a family man is the best worker. He has to be. I don't think you'll have trouble qualifying."

Angélique did not know the cruising range of the *Angélique* on a tank one-eighth full of fuel in the absence of wind. "I'm glad we've got water enough," Narcisse said. "We'll go to New Orleans, but first there are lots of things to get out of this hulk before a wind comes up and I have to put space between us." She did not know how hard he was praying for a wind. Not water now but fuel was essential, lest the *Angélique* drift becalmed in freakish doldrums till all the tanks were empty and all aboard her died, adding their insignificant twelve to the hundreds of millions already dead. Balancing his fears, he knew that if this fate were to become imminent he would go ashore no matter how hostile it looked, taking his rifle and pistol, and face whatever was there; and he made a red mark on the fuel gauge and swore to himself, When it gets down to there I'll beach us, yes, by God! He would aways save enough fuel to get to the beach.

He spent the rest of the day looting the hulk, taking everything useable that the *Angélique* could carry: electric cords, spare tools, nuts and bolts from the engine room, light bulbs, spare canvas for sails, denim dungarees and T-shirts, hemp lines and steel cables, oil cans, lubricating oil, till the deck of the *Angélique* looked like a Navy Surplus store.

"There isn't much for you, I'm afraid," he said to Angélique. "Remember, everything above four feet is gone. There's not even a dress. That sort of thing was all in the upper cabins."

"I don't think I could have worn it anyway, Narcisse."

He thought who might have worn it last, now atomized in the sunsets.

"No, I don't think I'd have liked you to."

His last transfer was curious, a case of champagne, a gesture of thanks to the derelict. When the sun set again he started the motor and drew away from the hulk till it was out of sight. Angélique chilled a bottle of champagne, on her part too a gesture of gratitude to their dead benefactors, the beverage they seemed to have celebrated with, and they popped its cork after the children were put to bed.

Neither of them was used to the insidious blandness of the bubbly stuff and they went to bed giggling. "I'm too tired to navigate tonight," he said. "No use putting up the sail in a calm. We'll drift till morning."

Towards morning Angélique nudged him. "Narcisse, the baby's crying. I'm going to see what's the matter."

"Eh?" said Narcisse.

Then he felt a crunch outside the hull and was instantly on deck, the motor going, his searchlight piercing through a light mist, beyond which shone a dim red nail-paring of a moon. In other years in other waters he would have expected a storm. But the barometer stood at its steady 30.04 as it had for days, and the sea was chilly and calm.

He had drifted into an elaborate but totally wrecked marina, all the floating parts of which, scorched and desolate, had drifted out to sea. His searchlight picked out the remains of the attendant's office, its door swinging open and shut with the swell. He saw the burnt skeleton of a gasoline pump. There was no more sleep for him that night.

At dawn he went aboard the wreck. Whatever blast had struck the marina had passed very quickly. There was a tank of gasoline beneath the pump and it had not exploded. Where there is service for gasoline boats there is service for diesel boats. He looked around and saw the thing he sought, the thing whose absence had given him waking nightmares. He shouted to Angélique, "Angélique! Angélique! Oil! Oil! Fuel oil!" He rushed back aboard.

"Angélique!"

Angélique was in the cabin feeding the baby.

"Angélique, we can cruise to the moon under power now! There's diesel oil enough for a tanker!"

She looked worried. He thought it was fatigue or some bad aftertaste of the champagne. He seized a sledge hammer, cold chisel and bucket and went down the jacob's ladder to the marina. The diesel pump, a complex electrical mechanism that metered and pumped the fuel, had been toppled and the hose was destroyed. But the fuel was there, the fuel was there! It sang like a song in his heart.

He broached the steel tank with a blow of his chisel, drew off a bucketful of the precious stuff and stoppered the hole, using the chisel as a bung. It leaked a little, but there was plenty more. He worked all day like a madman, not pausing to eat or drink. His shoes and dungarees dripped oil and he fouled the deck of the *Angélique* with it, but he did not care. Angélique forgot whatever had been bothering her and, with the help of the older boys, formed a bucket brigade, funneling it into the tank until, towards evening, the gauge read "full."

Then he paused, wondering what else on the *Angélique* could be used to hold oil. All the water casks were full and he was loath to empty even one of them.

"I could use your pots and pans," he said, laughing.

"No, thank you, dear." She was laughing too by now.

"Did you know how low we were, how bad it was?"

"Not really, but I had an inkling. You looked worried, even after the water."

"You looked worried about the baby. Is she sick?"

"I'll tell you about that," she said, thoughtfully.

"Not now. Tell me when I come back. I've got an idea. Unless she's sick. Is she?"

"Far from it."

"I'll be back in a minute."

This time he took a length of sturdy line and went aboard the marina. There was a fifty-gallon steel drum of lubricating compound there, a solid, heavy grease. It was nearly full, and he scooped it all out, having no use for it. Then the drum had to be flushed out with kerosene. He was not back in a minute. It took a whole hour. Then he made a sling in the end of the rope and heaved the free end aboard the *Angélique*. Angélique bent it around the rail to hold it fast.

"I'm coming aboard now," Narcisse called. "We'll all tail on and bring it to the deck. Then I'll fill it."

He, Angélique and the big boys pulled up the heavy drum and Narcisse eased it onto the deck. Then he filled it, bucketful by bucketful, till again he was ready to drop with fatigue.

"I'd stay for more," he said, glancing around the untidy deck, "but there's no room for more." Never had the *Angélique* looked so dirty and cluttered, nor had she had such an Ark-like supply of stores.

They sponged the worst of the oil off themselves with kerosene and finished with a bath of sea water and salt-water soap. Then Narcisse swabbed down the deck, for the oil and grease presented a fire hazard.

Then he had time to think, and he ate his first meal that day as he steered away. The sad thought struck him how much there is of everything in the world, how useless it is unless there are people, and how hard it is to procure things when there are no people to help you. He was, of course, desperately tired but he felt hopeful.

"Angélique," he said, "what worried you about the baby?"

"She has always worried me. She looks so *old*."

"Oh, I don't know."

"And she acts so old."

"I don't think there's anything wrong with that. She's just a little advanced over the others. Like her teeth. But both the doctor and Archange told us that's not so unusual."

"Narcisse, she was looking out of the porthole before we hit the marina. She cried *before* we bumped into it, as if she sensed danger."

"But there wasn't any danger. It was a dead calm. We

could have jolted against the thing all night and not even scraped the paint."

"But how could she see anything? It was foggy and dark. She must have eyes like a cat."

Narcisse frowned. It had indeed been dark, except for the bit of moon. "Maybe when the marina got very close she saw some dim shape and it frightened her. It doesn't seem likely but it might have happened."

"The noise was so soft when we hit, you'd have slept right through it, I think. I know I would have if Angélique hadn't wakened me with her crying."

"No, I always wake up when there's any unusual noise. I can sleep through the motor and the wind but anything like a bump wakes me up."

"She wouldn't have been telling us there was oil there, would she?"

Narcisse laughed heartily. "Well, you *are* worried, aren't you! Let's have a look at her."

They went into the cabin where Angélique was lying in her crib. She opened her big brown eyes and smiled.

"Well, young lady," Narcisse said, affecting a gruff voice of reproach, "you're causing your mother a great deal of worry. From now on you're going to behave like everybody else, nice and simple. Is that clear?"

"You're scaring her, Narcisse. You always do when you scold her. She doesn't know it's in fun." Little Angélique had drawn down the corners of her mouth and looked as if she were going to cry.

"There, there, bébé," Narcisse said, patting her head. "I didn't mean it. Don't be so sensitive. It's all right."

The child smiled hesitantly, brightening.

"It was very nice of you to call us when you saw the marina. Very nice indeed. Maybe you smelled the oil, eh? Well, we certainly needed it."

One baby eye closed and quickly opened again and little Angélique cooed with pleasure.

"Narcisse, she winked at you!"

"Nonsense; there's something in her eye."

But he looked and there wasn't. The baby sighed and snored off to sleep and the incident ended in laughter.

"She acts normal to me," Narcisse said. "Smart for her age maybe, more sensitive than the others, that's all. That's not bad, is it?"

"I guess I was just on edge," Angélique said.

Every day Narcisse sighted more ships, all steaming south. Through his glasses he sought in vain for national flags. He saw not one. Occasionally he would see the familiar old United Nations standard with its globe and wreath, but for the most part there were no flags at all. Nations still existed, for he heard them referred to on the New Orleans radio; but in the colossal work in which they were now of necessity engaged their separateness was forgotten, their identities merged, and the whole world took it for granted that they were united.

As he listened to the radio, sifting and evaluating the newscasts, he lost his enthusiasm for New Orleans. It was a city in transition; it served no purpose but to recruit and dispatch workers to Central America where The Dam was being built.

Narcisse was alive to the almost insuperable difficulty of constructing so enormous a project. "There will be millions of workers. It will take years. It is a job for a generation. Cities will have to be built, all dedicated to this one undertaking. I'll be old, I'll be dead before it is finished. But the whole area will be safe and well policed. It is the only place where my family can grow up under order, security and law. There will be good schools. There won't be enough houses at first, so maybe they'll let me live on my *Angélique*. Then, if things get better, I'll build us a house and I will go back to fishing for whatever fish have migrated to these waters." He looked at the water. He was off the Florida Keys. A strong current swept west and south towards the gap that had been the Isthmus of Panama, and flowed, as he now knew, into the Pacific. The water was chilly. Good, he thought. Again the cod. I know cod.

"Angélique," he said, "I am not going into the Gulf. We are not going to New Orleans. They would only send me to Central America anyway, and they might confiscate the boat. New Orleans is just a recruiting station."

Angélique nodded. "I've been listening too," she said. "It's like one big want ad; mechanics, truck drivers, electricians, engineers, everybody's needed. It says New Orleans is safe, but then they broadcast a long list of missing persons from the police station. Children get lost, men disappear. It's a parade going through and there's never a word about schools."

But the radio painted a glowing picture of the growing communities sprouting up at the termini of The Dam.

"We'll go to The Dam," Narcisse said; and he started south, like all the other ships.

He was glad he had made his decision, for somewhat later New Orleans itself was besieged by thousands of hungry refugees from the continental north, fleeing the cold; for always, creeping down from the poles, came The Big Ice, obliterating in its path the good, the bad, the opportunists, the victims, the preyed upon, the predatory, all, all in its path, frozen. In fact, conditions beyond Central America were for some years notorious for their savagery. In those days only the protected vicinity of The Dam was safe and reasonably normal in the planetary disruption of climate. As for the refugees who besieged New Orleans, since they were sick and half-mad and hence useless, it was necessary to shoot them, as in all cases where they threatened anything essential to The Dam, and they added their dismal toll to the two hundred million dead of The Twenty Minute War.

Narcisse steered a course towards Leon in Nicaragua, the busy metropolis on the northern terminus of The Dam. This city, formerly ten miles from the coast, now stood by the sea. Here the cancerous fires that ate up the earth had stopped, and past its seared and crystallized coast the Gulf Stream that no longer warmed the Atlantic poured unimpeded into the Pacific. Here was the northern end of The Dam, now just beginning. From here, for seven hundred miles, an obstruction to the sea would be built.

The *Angélique* was helped somewhat by the current, and once again a breeze had begun to blow from northeast to southwest, which also helped. But the problem of diesel oil still worried Narcisse and he was determined to keep his tanks full. How could he know, how could anyone know whether the breeze would hold?

Throughout the Caribbean there was a great deal of ship traffic, but the ships never stopped when he signalled them. They were driving full steam on their missions. When he got close, they whistled him out of the way and would have run him down if he had not scurried out of their path.

He hoped to find another derelict and replenish his supplies. Once he saw one, rusting now and bleached by fire. A patrol plane saw it too and instantly bombed it to the bottom. It was a menace to navigation.

On a desolate rocky isle he saw the wreck of another ship.

Since it was not a menace to navigation it had not been bombed. He drew close and examined it with his glasses. There were signs of life aboard, and presently a man in the last stages of starvation waved weakly to him and cried loudly in some foreign tongue and made motions for him to come aboard. Narcisse steered away from the craft. The fellow screamed and shook his bony fists and then collapsed on the deck, which Narcisse could see him pounding.

From that time he saw no more wrecks and assumed that they had either been sunk or swept into the Pacific by the current. Towards the end of the voyage it was necessary to ration the water.

That night he saw a glow in the sky, and for a moment he feared that the war had flared up again. But it was not the war; it was a concentration of searchlights on the construction at Leon, and the next morning he was met by a police boat. An apparently polyglot official questioned him, eyed the *Angélique* and its large human cargo and smiled tightly.

"You have come a long way, Monsieur Bolduc. Most people don't make it so far. Any sickness?"

"No, m'sieur."

"And dead? Did you lose any?"

"No, by God!"

"You are to be congratulated."

The official scrutinized him. Narcisse had lived all his life in the open and was young, bronzed and strong.

"Can you drive a bulldozer?"

Narcisse hesitated.

"If you can drive a trawler from the Gaspé here, you can drive a bulldozer," he decided. "Later we'll put you to piloting something. Right now we need bulldozer men. Do you have any arms? Rifles? Pistols? Anything that shoots?"

"Ye-es, sir."

"I'll take them, if you don't mind."

Narcisse watched him throw them overboard.

"No one is permitted arms any more except the police. Sorry."

Angélique and the children, ranged in steps down to the smallest who could stand, watched him.

"For the present you will live aboard your boat," he said. "You seem to have quite a brood. There isn't sufficient housing yet ashore, but we expect to have more soon. Please follow my boat. We'll berth you in the lagoon. It's what used to be the Lago de Nicaragua. You'll have a lot of company. It's a regular floating village, like the river communities in China—like they were, anyhow. Most of your neighbors are pleasant people; they came from everywhere. Do you drink?"

"Drink?"

"Drink liquor? Get drunk?"

Narcisse laughed.

The official looked at the family. "No, I suppose not. You've hardly had the time *or* the money."

"No, sir, I don't drink."

"Drinking isn't really prohibited, you know, but don't overdo. You have to show up every day for work, early, long hours, seven days a week. The penalty for absenteeism is severe. We withdraw protection and exile the unfit. I really don't know what happens to them. Conditions everywhere but at The Dam are very bad."

"I have seen those conditions."

The official held out his hand. "I think you will do very nicely." He gave him an identification card. "You will sign for any supplies you need at the Central Commissary till you're paid. Your card will be your credit. They will tell you in the office where to report for work. Au 'voir, mon brave."

Narcisse followed the boat into the lagoon and the *Angé-lique* tied up at a wharf for the first time since leaving the Gaspé.

His eldest boy asked, "Why did he throw away the guns, mon père? They were good ones, and I wanted to learn to shoot."

Narcisse said thoughtfully, "I don't think you'll ever shoot a gun as long as you live. There's been too much of it, and it's gone out of style."

CHAPTER 12

DURING the early stages of the reconstruction, when the engineering mistakes were made, Narcisse drove a bulldozer, hacking a feeder highway through a Nicaraguan jungle. Over that highway rolled, bumper to bumper, endless convoys of dump trucks, upending their loads of rock into the sea, while the *Angélique*, with his family aboard, rode gently on the sheltering surface of the lagoon, snugly fast to the wharf.

Narcisse was away when a tank truck came alongside to siphon off his diesel oil. "We'll need that," the driver said, presenting an authoritative card of some sort.

Angélique protested, "We can't live in the dark. We need it for the generator."

"They'll be bringing in shore power in a day or two," the man said calmly. "Sorry, lady," and he drained the tank. "You didn't have much," he said.

Each week Narcisse brought home his pay in the new currency, which was backed not by gold but by hours of work done on The Dam. Clouds of helicopters swarmed overhead dusting the atmosphere with DDT to kill the mosquitoes and penicillin to kill the cholera germs. A network of supply routes by land, sea and air fed and clothed the growing supply of workers.

At first they simply dumped rock into the sea, bonding it with water-hardening cement and asphalt. But this would not do, not nearly, though the jetties grew more rapidly than anything man had ever built before, stretching out from the shore, triumphantly dividing the waters. It looked slender from a distance, especially from the air. Actually it was a massive structure, with a multiple highway on top, firmly anchored at the base. At night (for the work never ceased) it was brilliantly illuminated. Smooth and powerful and solid, it held. But it was all too slow. New techniques, new machines were needed.

Omaha had been abandoned. Its vast underground shelters were no longer needed and the weather was Labradorean above ground. The United World Chiefs of Staff, under whose dictatorial discipline The Dam was being constructed had reassembled in Dallas and studied the logistics of the enterprise. On the basis of the work so far done they programmed their computers. The report was ominous: "At this rate it will take three hundred years to replace the matter which was destroyed. We do not enjoy that margin of time against The Big Ice."

Then came the monster diggers, earth movers as big as skyscrapers, that waded out into the sea up to their predetermined depth, their control cabins just above water level. They let down their steel snouts, gnawed at the ocean floor, fused it with electrical heat and deposited it in forty-ton bricks, pre-formed, still steaming, into the body of The Dam.

Still it was not enough, though the work went faster, for as yet The Dam was being constructed from only two ends, namely, the Colombian and the Nicaraguan termini.

A totally new aproach was needed, even if it meant scrapping all the specially constructed diggers; and since it was an ocean problem, the oceanographers were again asked to present a plan.

Academician Anapolskoi said, "We must rebuild the Isthmus as if we were Anthozoan polyps, and we must build in many places at once. There is no other way. They begin on the ocean floor and build upwards towards the surface." He pointed to the Great Barrier Reef of Australia, a coral growth far longer than the seven hundred miles of destroyed Central America. "You have been trying to build from the top down, like building a house roof first instead of the foundation first. Nature teaches us the right way—trees, corals, the very mountains, organic and inorganic, they all begin at a lower level and grow upwards in stature."

He was enormously respected. His word carried weight. And there was a strong feeling, verging on superstition, that some natural way of healing the wound in the earth ought to be found, since the burning of the Isthmus smote men's conscience as an affront against Nature, and Nature was exacting a horrible vengeance in the northern latitudes. Thus it was that a second engineering mistake was made.

Giant caissons were constructed and lowered beneath the waves. In them crews of sandhogs labored in continuous shifts, playing upon the ocean floor a constant stream of cement from huge flexible steel hoses that came down from supply ships on the surface, providing a base for The Dam. These pressurized bell jars worked in a string of seventy isolated locations where the water was most shallow. The Dam was being rebuilt not only from two widely separated termini but simultaneously all along its projected course.

The principle was sound. But the World Chiefs of Staff, feeding the logistics into their computers and reading the invariable answer, "One hundred years," held grave and secret consultations. They knew, though as yet no one else did, that a monstrous error had been made. Given time, this method of construction would have succeeded. Slowly, polyplike, along the vast arc where the Isthmus had been, in seventy "cells" spotted at ten-mile intervals, the base of The Dam was beginning to rise from the ocean floor. Beavers too, dumb brutes, can build dams, given time enough. But for Man there was no time. What he had destroyed in a day he must rebuild in a day, and those who knew the secret kept it, wondering how. Meanwhile, for the toiling hordes engaged in their forlorn venture, there was an upsurge of hope and good feeling. No one had ever worked so long, so hard, so enthusiastically. Despite everyone's constant fatigue, the night clubs and theaters were full. Radio reports of each day's progress were greeted with cheers. The papers published optimistic charts, showing each foot of rise. Those who asked, "Why don't they give a completion date?" were silenced with frowns and accused of having no faith and ceased to ask questions. At heart everyone was afraid to think about the possibility of failure. Sociologists have called this frenetic euphoria in the midst of an obviously hopeless enterprise one of the oddest periods of the reconstruction of the Isthmus.

Bill Young's destroyer was converted into a giant cement mixer. Her turrets, torpedoes, bombs, shells, guns and all other heavy armament had long since been heaved overboard to supply bulk and bonding for the bottom of The Dam. Her only function now was to mix cement and pipe it down into the caissons at the bottom. Then, relinquishing her place at the head of the line, she would steam back to port for another load. There were no leaves or furloughs for the military, no vacations for the civilian workers. For long periods of time neither Bill Young, who had risen to Commander, nor Narcisse Bolduc, who had risen to a Construction Chief, saw their families, and when they did it was for a very brief rest. They marveled at their children's growth, and they wished The Dam would grow as fast.

Narcisse, after the first phase when he had driven the bulldozer, was now in charge of an enormous mechanized scow which provided air and electricity to one of the seventy steel caissons. These service scows had been rapidly cast of reinforced concrete and were crammed with machinery. It had been realized that a man who could pilot a fishing trawler from Canada to Central America, encumbered with ten children, was fearless and adept at improvisation. Narcisse and Commander Young did not know each other's names, but they knew and respected each other's skills. Young's destroyer would sometimes service the caisson that Narcisse's scow provided with power and air. The scow commander admired the rapidity with which the destroyer pumped down its load, and the destroyer commander admired the seamanship with which the scow commander kept his heavy craft out of the way of the destroyer without drifting too far or snapping his metal lines. They were about of an age; they knew each other by sight, and each would grin a greeting when their craft worked together and say to himself, Well, I won't have to trouble with this one. He knows his business. It was always a good day when they met. Narcisse would go home to the *Angélique*—he had not yet acquired a house—and Young would go home to the cottage he had helped build, and their wives would find them less tired and in a better humor than usual.

More than a year had passed and the Gulf Stream still flowed on its unimpeded course into the Pacific. The climate of Central America seemed very pleasant to all newcomers. The nights were cool and the days were balmy and warm.

It had been a perpetual springtime. But those who had lived there all their lives complained of increasing cold. Many were miraculously cured of the wasting tropical diseases they had always taken for granted, only to come down with pneumonia and vicious virus colds, which they had never known before.

There was increasing dismay among the World Chiefs of Staff. No matter how hopefully the computers were programmed, the completion date still came out as the months went by in a distressing series of answers: 99.9 years more, 99.8—and after two years and one month the answer was 99.001. The reason it was distressing was simply that it was so accurate.

Newspaper and radio reports had been severely censored from the beginning. Now it was necessary to clamp down an absolute blackout of news about the northern latitudes. Whole cities had frozen. The migrant refugees had fought among themselves and swarmed like destroying locusts on cities farther south. There had been wholesale exterminations. But there had been escapes also, and some of them had made their way to the megalopolis that had grown up around The Dam. One could not shoot them merely because they brought bad news, so the tales were told of the horrors of The Big Ice, and grew with the telling.

As, one by one, the northern industrial centers shut down— for not all were hit—a shortage came about of many essential materials for building The Dam, especially steel and heavy electrical machinery. The spirit of the workers began to flag, and their original euphoria passed. There was less DDT to kill the mosquitoes now and less medicine: the chemical plants were gone. There was a shortage of surgical tools. No new houses were built because all lumber from the north was unprocurable now and no one made cement blocks because all cement had been commandeered for The Dam.

The computers now gave the expected completion date, "99.000 more years."

This figure, which amounted to a sentence of death, if not for the human race at least for civilization, was not released at the time. But it was at this juncture that the World Chiefs of Staff, who had now set up headquarters in New Orleans, issued their famous order. It was cloaked in obscure phraseology. It said: "All persons living within twenty miles of The Dam will evacuate for a period of three days to a distance of at least fifty miles except personnel designated for special duty. There are no exceptions. You will have ten days to effect the evacuation. Every transportation help will be afforded those who cannot supply their own. Persons not obeying this order cannot be protected, nor will any attempt on the part of the authorities be made to do so."

So as not to alarm the populace there was a cryptic explanation: "A radically new technique to expedite construction will be attempted. After that you are to return to your homes and work will proceed as usual."

The doom in the last sentence, the possibility of failure, was felt only by the desperate inner circle of the World Chiefs of Staff.

This order lifted much of the gloom from the populace and the evacuation became a holiday, a holiday no one had had for two years.

Betty Young said to Bill, "I'm glad they're going to try something new. It's seemed such a long time."

"Part of the trouble," Bill said, "is that all the work's being done under water. Nobody can see any progress. When they build a building you can see it go up story by story, but with The Dam you can't see an inch of progress. It's actually going pretty well."

Bill Young, Jr., who had walked at six months, looked at him disgustedly and said, "Huh!"

The youngster troubled his father. Many children speak a bit at the age of two, but this one seemed to have a remarkable vocabulary and his enunciation was crystal clear, without a trace of childish lisp, probably because he had cut all his teeth so early.

"I'll be glad of the holiday," Betty said. "It's so long since I've seen you more than a day at a time. We'll take a trip up in the hills. They're all green again, Bill. It will be like Jamaica."

Bill said, "Yes, you go, dear, and take the boy. But I'm afraid I can't go with you. I've been ordered out on a special mission."

"Oh no! Then it won't be a holiday at all."

"No, Betty, it's not, not really. They've made it sound pretty casual, because if the new technique doesn't work they don't want to worry people."

"Bill, you look terribly serious."

"If it fails, it's pretty nearly the end of everything."

"But you just said progress on The Dam was going well."

"That's what I tell everybody, and so must you. But you see—you see—well, anything that can speed it up a bit is all to the good, and—"

"Bill?" she said, stopping him short. She could always tell when he was hiding something.

He sighed. "All right, dear, I'll tell you the truth. Don't spread it around. We're going to set off some underwater nuclear bombs. They're going to fight fire with fire."

Bill Young, Jr. nodded his two-year-old head and said

vehemently, "I should have thought that would have occurred to the blockheads in charge at the very outset."

"Oh, keep quiet," Bill said. On rare occasions the boy came out with a long remark like that and it always gave him the creeps.

"Bill, if you can't come, Bill Jr. and I will hitch a ride with the Bolducs."

"Who are they?"

"A Canadian family who live on an old fishing boat. He's a scow engineer. They've a huge family and they're hiring three station wagons. There'll be plenty of room, and they're very nice."

It was better than sending her off in the car alone, or taking one of the crowded public conveyances.

"That sounds all right," he said.

It drizzled during the night. Next morning as Commander Young went to his ship, now stocked with nuclear bombs about the size of basketballs, he saw a scrap of paper in the grass. It contained several lines, and the first was printed in a childish hand. It contained four words. These four words were repeated five or six times in succeeding lines, each line a little better looking. The last line might have been printed by a competent letterer. The words were, "Fight fire with fire."

It would be Bill Young, Jr., again, always ahead of himself, now trying to write. He had, of course, heard his father say the words last night.

Then it occurred to Commander Young that his son had not been out of the house last night, and the scrap of paper looked as if it had lain there for days. He grew angry at the thought and denied the tingling down his spine. No. The youngster had practiced with a pencil after he went to bed. He was always waking up at night. He seemed to sleep very little. He had experimented with a pencil and pad and the wind had blown the paper out of the window.

When Betty and Bill Jr. joined the caravan of station wagons, Narcisse, whose new English still had a Gallic cast, greeted her warmly. "What is two more?" he said, grinning. "Me, I could take four. You honor us with your company, Madame Young, also the p'tit bébé. And you can help with the housework, non?"

"Of course I will, Mr. Bolduc."

"My husband isn't needed for the blasting," Angélique said to her. "It's going to be our first real holiday in two years. It will be heavenly. I only wish it were longer. I still don't know what stopped work on The Dam."

"Oh," said Narcisse, "everybody knows that now. It comes by the vineyard."

Angélique whispered, "He means grapevine."

"They're going to blow up a big cordon of mountains and build The Dam in one day. Some big engineer in the World Chiefs figured it out."

"I'd consider that a most sensible solution," said little Angélique, looking gravely at Bill Young, Jr.

"My bébé, she learn English quicker than me," Narcisse said proudly. "Goddam smart little bébé, non?"

Betty looked uneasily at the children.

"I'm afraid they both are," she said.

PART THREE

THE INTRUDERS

CHAPTER 1

THERE was no longer time for palliative measures. No margin for error remained. Under a blanket of heavy snow which was rapidly hardening into solid ice the northern latitudes were uninhabitable. The Great Lakes were frozen. In lower latitudes where palms had once flourished, the northern pine had now begun to grow. With the passing of each day, each year, it had become apparent that, without recourse to some radical experiment, a man-made Glacial Age would terminate or reduce to the level of brutes the whole of mankind.

It was then that the United World Chiefs of Staff gave orders to blast. No one knew whether the experiment would succeed. Some prophets of doom voiced a warning that the earth, having barely recovered from one sensitizing sting of the new bombs, was now allergic to them, and that any further infection would constitute an anaphylactic sting, on the analogy of the violent reaction some people have to one bee sting and then die at the second: and that the planet would simply consume itself in one giant flare, leaving behind not so much as a thimbleful of ash. The prophets of doom were voted down. As between an experiment that

177

might end in instantaneous extinction by fire, along with those other two hundred million mortals, but that promised hope, contrasted with sitting idly by to await slow death by freezing of the majority and brutalization of the remnant, there was no choice. The blast was decreed, with all its perils.

Throughout the length of the serpentine sea of emptiness where Central America had been, a double row of small clean nuclear bombs were planted on the ocean floor. While the whole world held its breath, and many prayed, these bombs were detonated by a radar signal. In a grim and solemn ceremony, televised over the globe, the (provisional) President of the United States and the (provisional) Premier of the USSR pressed with their fingers, having first shaken hands, an ivory button that sent out the signal. The detail was noted that this button was made of fossil ivory from the tusk of a Siberian mammoth. The brute had been found intact, flowers undigested in its stomach, in a bog that had suddenly frozen fifty thousand years ago in a similar never-explained climatic change. No one denied the appropriate-ness of such ivory. If man too were about to disappear, with a vanishing planet, let it be with dignity and consciousness that he had brought his fate upon himself, a self-appraisal of which the brute mammoth was incapable, not being a man. In the greater mystery that has come upon us since that cere-mony and the perils that now assail us, it is well to remem-ber that the silly world of man faced that moment of instant and universal annihilation with courage that touched on divinity.

The desperate decision to reconstitute The Dam by blast-ing was brilliantly successful. At the touch of the button, forthwith, once again, the midnight sky blazed with a fiery white glow as seven hundred underwater nuclear bombs detonated simultaneously. But this time they did not destroy; they built. This time they did not kill; they saved.

When the thunder rolled away and the waves were spent and the fire was out and the sea was smooth again there was seen, still steaming and hissing, but healthy and firm like an infant new born and glad to breathe fresh air, a seven-hundred-mile stretch of earth, the biggest dike ever piled up by man, torn from the bottom of the ocean, standing like a ridge between two furrows of plowed field. This colossal feat required less than sixty seconds, the explosion time of the bombs, in its final achievement.

Fire had been fought with fire. Infection had been conquered by a counterirritant. The configuration of the ocean floor was as it had been two years before, and a Panama Isthmus once more was in being.

All the sick symptoms of earth's torture began to reverse themselves. The Gulf Stream, dammed by the artificial Isthmus, was blocked from its central passage into the Pacific and now doubled back upon itself in its former course and carried its beneficent heat to Europe and all the northern latitudes. The Humboldt Current began again its accustomed orbit of the Pacific. In the Gobi Desert no more red rain fell and in North America the Great Lakes began to thaw, starting with the southernmost, Lake Michigan, in the area of Chicago Bay, the great estuary where once the city had stood. Normality seemed to have been restored and, as fleets of reconnaissance planes fanned out to take the temperature of the northern latitudes, confirmation flooded in that it had. The earth sickness had lasted two years and three months before the successful solution was found, not a very long time as human history is measured, a mere tick of the cosmic clock in the life span of a planet.

But history is a spiral, never a circle, and nothing ever

quite returns to the place where it starts. No sick person is ever, after recovery, quite the same as he was before the sickness struck him, and neither was the planet. Only the climate was cured.

It will now be right to return to the account of the short life of Wilson Young, Jr., who was born during the glare of the nuclear holocaust that constituted The Twenty Minute War; to relate how he grew to precocious manhood, wiser at twenty than the common run of men at fifty; how at that tender age he was brutally murdered and how the threat of retaliation for his murder hangs over the world like overshadowing bat wings of some dark and intruding angel of death, beyond passion and beyond our poor power of science or prayer to exorcise. And it is only fitting to disclose that the author of this narrative is his father, Commander Wilson Young, Sr., writing a memorial to his only child, a son with a sweet and oddly innocent nature. He never did a bad or ugly thing. I do not think he ever had a bad or ugly thought, though my standards were not his and I am not at all sure how he thought. To me his mental processes will always remain a mystery. Yet in paying my tribute to my child I must at the same time voice a warning against his alarming gifts, which evoke both admiration and apprehension in men like me, who do not share those gifts.

I had always hoped Bill would look like me and think like me. In my great sorrow since his death I have sought the advice of experts in emotional matters, for I could not put down a feeling of guilt that this desire might have been overpossessive.

In my special position as his father I was naturally a subject of clinical interest and investigation, not all of it friendly. I have been tested by tests I could not understand

and interrogated by psychiatrists, sociologists, geneticists and policemen, whose very vocabulary I could not fathom. Well, I did understand the policemen. These scientists were prominent men. Their yearly salary would equal ten of mine. It will be seen in its proper place why they took such pains to interrogate me. I'm afraid I disappointed them, however. One and all they pronounced me quite ordinary; and the most renowned of them, completing a fat dossier on my boy, said to me, "I can learn nothing from you, Commander Young. You are transparently incapable of faking all these normal reactions." He flipped through the results of a test he had given me. "One doubts if you could really be his father." I grew angry, and he smiled. "Yes, even that flush of fury, quite, quite normal." He held out his hand, as well he might, in a conciliatory gesture, and I was willing to shake it. Let these supercerebral psychiatrists know that Commander Young does not hold science against them, I of all people. "Ah well," he said, "we must seek further, further than you." And he, like all the others, assured me that my desire for Bill to be like me was not overpossessive.

But Bill was not like me. He was not like anyone else I ever knew. He was more than me. He was, I think—indeed I fear, for he always frightened me—more than human, at least the humans I have known.

I was not aware that in many respects he was strange from the very beginning. The times were troubled and full of activity, troubled as they had never been before. I was away on my ship and, like everyone else, I was employed twelve hours a day on the building of The Dam. I saw very little of my wife and my boy. Future generations will find it difficult to imagine the state of mind, the tensions and fears under which we all lived during that critical period. The Dam crowded out every other thought, even of our own families. We worked like slaves and lived like ants, perpetually in motion, oblivious of surroundings. Narcisse Bolduc, the Canadian engineer who became my neighbor, has told me that he too, though his family was numerous, had little time to enjoy his children, so great was the press of our desperate labor.

Somewhat sentimentally I had, for example, visualized Bill's face some fine day when he would grow to adolescence, appearing over my shoulder when I was shaving, and he would say to me, "Hey, pop, gimme the loan of your razor, huh? I got a date." His face would be a younger version of mine, softened by youth and a mingling with Betty's. And I would hear myself replying with a wonderful air of paternal scorn but actually bursting with pride, "OK, go ahead, shave off the peach fuzz if you can see it and try not to slit your throat." But this never happened, nor anything like it. He never needed to shave and I never once heard him say "gimme" or use any other slang. He always talked like a speech instructor or some very precise, highly educated foreigner. This irked me, because I could never correct him, but it also made me proud. A father likes a smart son. He soon proved too smart—not in the sense of "smarty"; he was anything but that, but in the sense of "quick." It will be seen how self-conscious he made me feel in his presence, for I feel it even now; and I will always try to improve my speech because Bill once said to me, "Precise speech means precise thinking." He was about four years old when he said that.

Bill's voice changed at six, but he never broke out in adolescent pimples; his skin was always as fair and smooth as a baby's, and his large brown eyes retained to the day of his death the limpid luminous quality I had seen and marveled at in the hour when he was born. "Beauty" is not a word a father applies to a son, but even at the college locker-room stage there was a clarity and sweetness about my boy's face that I know no other word to describe. His forehead was fair and high; his hair was extraordinarily fine; he was tall and broad-shouldered and, though his frame was slight, every inch a man. He had a quick and competent walk and his spine was straight as an admiral's. His corpse was scientifically calibrated in millimeters and his head was the subject of much discussion by reason of its being somewhat larger than average. This will interest those who make such things their business. But this is how his father saw him: noble.

I can almost hear him now; and he would be reproaching me as I tell this tale: "Father, you encroach upon chronology." Actually, the thing that frightened me most about Bill was exactly that sort of irrefutable logic; for indeed I am running ahead of the strict sequence of events. Back then, dear dead, my son, to when you were four.

At that time The Dam was a year and eight months old, and The Big Ice was melting. Preparations were in train to rebuild the great northern civilizations. Fleets of reconnaissance planes were photographing the remains of cities, which could not be rebuilt because they were largely water-filled holes, spotting likely sites for new cities when the people would trek north again. The TV satellites, with their wider view of the recession of the snow, aided in this project; and the fertilization of the soil by reason of the dust contained in the snow, like the Nile in Egypt, was early recognized as a promise of bigger and better crops over a wider expanse of earth than had ever been known before. This, as is known, proved true. Never were farms so fertile nor food so plentiful as after the climatic change.

Though The Dam, as a dam, was performing its function,

it was universally conceded that it ought to be made stronger. It was at first only a reef, barren and, in spots, dangerous to navigation, with fortuitous jetties and unexpected concavities caused by the local explosions. I complained about this misdirection of some of the bomb charges, and Bill said to me, "Who expects a full-fledged Rodin when the workmen blast a quarry?"

I, of course, looked up Rodin and found that he was a famous sculptor and realized what Bill meant. He meant that as yet only the groundwork was done on The Dam, and that to be civilized and meaningful the reconstructed Isthmus required refinement. Bill's remark was sharp and compact, but as soon as I caught his meaning I did not think it especially remarkable. We all knew that eventually The Dam would be a complicated and beautiful piece of engineering, with canals through it to facilitate navigation between the oceans, railways and highways over it to establish ground communication between the Americas, and a complex of power plants and habitations, perhaps even cities, for those who would man it. Bill, as usual, put it all in a few impatient words, which seemed patronizing in a child of four.

Betty took him for an outing in one of the spacious new parks that were being built on the first broad mile of the land end of The Dam. It was a recreational area full of restaurants and theatres for adults, and playgrounds for children of all ages. There were broad lawns and wonderfully landscaped gardens. It was high noon and a sunny day, the temperature about seventy-five. Mornings were still chilly, of course, as were the evenings, but the midday temperatures had begun to approach the ideal. She had dressed him in a topcoat, knowing that he reacted adversely to the fog and the cold of the mornings. She was not prepared for his sudden reaction to the noonday sun as the temperature rose. He sweated and became irritable and took off his coat and loosened his tie, breathing uncomfortably.

"Well, I'd have done the same," I said. "Seventy-five is summer heat and anybody would take off a topcoat."

Bill showed no interest in the seesaws and swings that would have appealed to an ordinary four-year-old boy, but he was elated by the chute-the-chutes and went down the slide again and again on the seat of his britches, whooping for joy and landing with amazing agility. Most kids tumble and roll like pumpkins or come smacking down on their bottoms, but Bill, after one try, landed on his feet with knees expertly bent like a trained ski jumper. "He has a magnificent sense of balance," Betty said.

After the first exhilaration of the slide, when he had mastered it, he lost interest in it. "That was delightful," he said. His face was flushed and happy, his eyes sparkling.

"We'll come back and do it again," Betty said.

"But I've already done it," he said, looking perplexed.

"But if it was fun you'll want to do it again," Betty said.

"Oh I see," he said, but the queer patronizing tone had crept into his voice. As a matter of fact, he never went back to the chute-the-chutes.

There was also on that day the child's toy called a Jungle Jim. It was a pyramidal construction of ordinary plumbers' pipes, and its purpose was to encourage youngsters to gain muscular coordination. The top of the Jungle Jim was perhaps ten feet high. It was full of shouting youngsters, swinging and hanging and laughing, with T-shirts wet in the armpits from the sweat of their exercise. They laughed when Bill put his hands on the lowest rungs. "Hey, skinny! This ain't for kids," one said, warning him away, not unkindly.

His answer was, Betty said, " 'It seems to be, since kids

infest it.' I don't think they understood, but they scowled at him. He doesn't mix easily, Bill."

"Then he came down?"

"No. After a preliminary swing or two, as if he were getting the feel of the thing, he scampered up to the very top so fast I could hardly follow him with my eye. I was afraid he'd fall off."

"Obviously he didn't."

"No, he put his hands in his pockets, walked upright on the ridge bar like a tight-rope walker and scampered down again. I've never seen such a sense of balance."

"That ought to have put the other kids in their place."

"They were good kids. Some of them clapped and cried, 'Atta boy.' They were good little sports and encouraged him."

"What did Bill do?"

"He thumbed his nose at them and looked at them in absolute scorn."

"We'll have to teach him some manners," I said, chuckling.

It clouded up after noon and a summer squall came on with a thick, though short cover of clouds which quite obscured the sun. Betty took Bill for lunch. They sat by a big glass window overlooking a flower garden. Bill had a healthy appetite and ate fast, as he usually did.

"I told him it wasn't polite to eat so fast," Betty said.

"I always forget," he replied, and paced his manipulation of knife and fork to match hers.

Betty said, "I've the queerest feeling he watches us on the sly to see how we do things, as if he'd do them differently."

"Oh, I suppose all kids copy their parents. That's the way they learn."

"I suppose," she said; but I could see she was unconvinced.

Betty, who saw so much more of him than I, spotted many of his oddities sooner than I could.

I was not much concerned with his table manners or his thumbing his nose at the children below him while he walked unconcernedly on the bar at the dizzy top of the Jungle Jim; but then Betty told me something that really bothered me, since I greatly disliked mysteries. Alas, how many he demonstrated later on.

"There was a sundial in the garden," Betty said. "I told him how it worked: you read the shadow like the hand of a clock. He studied it a moment and then he said, 'I see. On that basis I'd say it's a little past one right now. Isn't it?'"

"Was it?"

"I had to look at my watch. It was one-fifteen."

"Pretty good," I said.

"Bill, there wasn't any shadow. It was raining cats and dogs and there wasn't any sun."

"Maybe he sneaked a look at your watch." We both knew he could already tell time. "I don't like sneaks."

"Maybe he did, but it would have been pretty hard for him to see."

She wore it habitually on the inside of her wrist, having got the habit when crystals were hard to get, and you break fewer of them in that position.

"Well then, he just made a lucky guess. Nobody can read a sundial when there's no shadow." But later I learned that Bill could.

"Bill?" she asked me.

"Yes? What now?"

"Bill, what kind of numbers do sundials have?"

I stopped and thought.

"Oh, good Lord!" I said.

"Yes," she said. "Did you ever teach him Roman numerals?"

"I hardly know them myself."

"Well, that sundial had Roman numerals."

"Then he was really guessing," I said.

Later—it was always later, that sickening word, far too much later—I learned that Bill knew all about Roman numerals; moreover, he had read the shadowless dial with unerring accuracy, since the shadow was there for him, as clear as if the stormy sky had been cloudless.

Bill had a serious case of sunburn next day, though Betty was only slightly tanned from her short exposure with him in the sun. It was painful, he blistered and he whimpered. The condition cleared up in a few days, sooner in fact than it does in most people; but we knew then and there that Bill was abnormally sensitive to sunburn in addition to his being intolerant of extremes of heat and cold. We had on our hands a delicate child who bore watching, lest, through our carelessness, some allergy do him real harm. But he himself took care of the matter and walked in the shade or covered himself with Betty's suntan oil when he went swimming. I cannot remember his ever being sunburned again. Bill never had to learn anything twice. That is why he bewildered us so at the beginning. He was always ahead of us. He always took care of himself, solving his own problems before we were aware of them. This elicits admiration but frustrates love, since you never can *do* anything for such people.

The next year he entered school. I would have put him in kindergarten, if only to slow him down; but he was tested with the latest tests and they skipped him several grades and at the age of five he was plumped down among ten- or eleven-year-olds. "Your son," came the report from the school, couched in that high academic jargon that no one can understand and that always bristles my hackles, "has demonstrated above median potential in terms of coordination, apprehension, adjustability to environment and ability to mentally structure unexplored areas of thought as presented by the advanced curricula," and it was recommended that he start among much older boys and girls.

"Is this a good report?" I asked Betty. All I could see was the split infinitive.

"Yes, it is."

"What is this thing about 'structure'?"

" 'Structure' is a new word teachers use nowadays. It means Bill can think concretely."

"Then it's a good report."

"Oh yes."

This seemed quite wrong.

I put on my dress uniform, thinking to impress the principal, and went to the school to protest. Bill was quite sufficiently advanced as it was. I believed at the time that I had a very bright boy, maybe even a prodigy, and I believed that prodigies rocketed up for a time and burnt out like spent rockets, coasted and plummeted into obscurity at an age when most men are just getting their start.

"Not at all," said the man at the school. He was not the principal; he was a kindly, personable psychologist who gave the tests. "The prodigies who burn out, as you put it, are the exception. Once a good brain, always a good brain; and for every burnt-out prodigy I can cite you fifty geniuses who begin early and end late, in full command of their faculties, having greatly enriched our culture."

"I'd like to rein him in," I said.

He said, "You would do him a great disservice. He will

stagnate if we don't challenge his potential. Now we don't want to do that, do we?"

He made me feel as if my dress uniform were wrinkled and lacked buttons.

"I just want him to be like everybody else," I said. "Like me."

"Oh, I'm afraid we can't have *that*," he said, and later, when I told Bill about the conversation, Bill seemed to be trying to hide a smile.

"He talked to me about the tests," Bill said, laughing. "I said I was good at ambition, distraction, uglification and derision. He said, 'Ah, you like mathematics. Good.' And he gave me a reading test."

I knew he could read.

"You passed, of course."

"He thanked you for teaching me how."

"Son, I never taught you. You must have picked it up, a word here and there, maybe traffic signs, headlines in the newspapers, I don't know. Lots of children do that. But I never taught you, not much anyhow."

"Do you mind that I gave you credit?" he asked, somewhat more seriously than usual.

"Certainly not," said I.

The psychologist also remarked at that interview, "You will note that Bill has a marvelous sense of humor: ambition, distraction, uglification and derision! So few read *Alice in Wonderland* nowadays to their children. Congratulations, Commander."

I hadn't.

"Well, I know Bill's bright," I said, "but I just don't want to push him. Put him among his—his—his—"

"Peers?" said the man. "His equals? That's what we're going to do."

"But they're too old."

"Are you sure, Commander, that Bill is only five? Physically and mentally our tests show he is at least ten." He looked at me as if I could not count beyond five.

"He was born in the middle of The Twenty Minute War," I said, "right in the middle, ten minutes after it started, ten minutes before it stopped. I certainly ought to know when he was born."

I thought his pleasant expression changed at that.

Bill was put in the advanced class. There was a great need for engineers and his tests proved that he possessed an innate grasp of mathematics. The schools were thinking far ahead to the reconstruction of great areas of devastated cities in the North; engineers would be needed for a generation, perhaps two, and a parent had little to say about the education of promising children. Their education was pushed, whether the parent liked it or not. Secretly, I suppose, I liked it. I like success and Bill was superbly equipped to succeed.

It was during this first year of school that he divulged the mystery of how he had read the sundial in the garden the year before. He came to me one day with his handsome face taut and intense. I had grown to dislike that look, and braced myself.

"Dad," he said, "can anybody see in the dark?"

"No," I said, irked. The school had called, telling me he was not in class, asking why he was absent. I had not known he was, but I had said, "He came home at noon with a bad headache." Perhaps I said stomach-ache, I don't know. I know I covered up.

"No," I said, "not even owls. I've been tested for that sort of thing, while we were building The Dam, when they wanted to know who had night vision. If it's really dark, no

matter what reputation they have, owls and cats and every·
thing else equipped with eyes, they can't see, not a thing.
Far less men. Now don't tell me you can. And why didn't
you go to class today? I had to lie for you."

"I got bored, but I didn't play hookey. I went to a science
lecture."

"Yes, son?"

I didn't want to scold him because of how he looked.

"Bees have ultraviolet vision," he said, as if that would explain everything. I boned up on the subject secretly and
found that it was true.

"That is very fine for the bees," I said.

He said, "So have I."

He said he had been able to see the sun that day when the
clouds were thick, a bright disc beyond the clouds; and for
him it cast a shadow on the sundial. "I didn't know Mama
couldn't see it," he said. "I thought everybody had ultraviolet vision."

"It would be best if you didn't mention this to anyone
else," I said after some thought. "People don't like people
who are different. If you can really see through clouds, sunlight when everybody else is in a fog—"

"Oh, I can."

"—well, just don't let on. People will think you're a—a—"

"Freak, dad?"

"I didn't say that."

"Freak?"

"No, gifted. They get jealous."

"Freak."

"Oh, stop it. Stop it!"

"I'll stop."

I was touched that he had come to me for guidance.

CHAPTER 2

HE came to me once more for guidance. He was ten years old at the time. It was the last time he ever asked my advice. Thereafter he did not need to, and, increasingly, I lost contact with him.

He said to me, "Dad, when did you start to shave?"

I thought back and, giving myself a couple of years' handicap for purposes of bragging, answered, "Well, I guess I started about your age, about ten, why?"

"I think that's about the right age," he said.

I cupped his smooth chin in my palm. There wasn't a trace of fuzz, although, oddly, his voice had already changed, without the squeaks and breaks that normally accompany sexual maturity, and was now a rich tenor, singularly pleasing.

"Yup," I said. "You'd better shave that chin."

Thereafter, dutifully, he shaved every third day, and kept a razor in his locker at school for the other boys, who actually needed to shave, to see.

I said to Betty, "I've seen him in swimming trunks and he hasn't any hair on his chest. It's curious he thinks he has to shave that smooth chin of his. I guess he just wants to keep up with the other boys."

She answered, "He has very scant pubic hair also."

I was shocked. "How in the world do you know?"

"He's very careless about taking his showers. I had to scold him. You don't walk around naked in front of women, even your own mother."

"Well, I should hope not!"

"He listened attentively and now he puts on a bathrobe like you, like everyone else. He has to *learn* the simplest things. I don't think he has any moral sense at all."

We both knew that certain highly educated, usually better-class parents, bathed in the nude in front of their youngsters, the purpose being to promote "adjustment" in the young; but we had never subscribed to this sort of so-called education. I objected because it was immodest; damn it, it was worse than that, it was downright dirty. Betty objected on esthetic grounds. "Why destroy their illusions?" she said. As usual, Betty and I were in agreement, though from a somewhat different approach to the subject: it was certainly not right to go back to a Garden-of-Eden nudity, not in the family. But here was Bill, innocent as our First Parents before they varied their diet, poor Bill who had to be told that we were civilized now and had progressed beyond all that! Perhaps he was born without a normal sense of guilt. Bill learned quickly, as he always did, and he was properly modest thereafter.

Bill achieved full growth at twelve, standing six-feet-two in his socks. The scientists who measured him in millimeters after he died no doubt placed on file in some anthropological institution a more accurate measurement, but this was enough for me. Betty would put a book on his head when he was growing, and make a mark on the wall with a pencil. The book was a cheap dictionary that I used to refer to in writing my reports, since the Admiral was always a stickler for correct spelling and my own left much to be desired.

Bill's attitude towards athletics seemed odd to me. He didn't give a damn. With his build I should have thought he would like sports. I always had.

"Bill," I said, "I can understand that you might not care much for boxing and football; you're rather slight for those sports." Candidly, I was afraid he'd be bashed to a pulp. "But what about tennis and squash or track? Maybe fencing, even. Or baseball?"

"Would that please you?" he said.

"Well, it's a lot of fun to win."

"Win what?" he said.

"Win the game!" I said harshly.

He thought a moment and answered, smiling, "Oh, I see. I'll do that."

He struck me as strangely sure of himself.

There followed a painful period. To please me he went out for baseball. Betty and I went to watch him. He was superbly coordinated. When he pitched the batter always struck out. When he was up at bat he belted in home runs as a matter of course, without apparent effort. His coach puzzled over his batting average and scratched his head and said to me, "Commander, nobody would believe this," and tore up the score. "It's freak luck."

I said, "Well, even if it is, you ought not to tear up the record."

He said, "I must have made a mistake."

"Aren't you even going to congratulate him?" I said.

"Oh sure, I'll congratulate him."

But Bill derived no sense of elation from his victories. They had come too easily. He had won without effort. The congratulations of the coach embarrassed him. He completely lacked the competitive spirit. He took his superiority for granted, marveling at the clumsiness of his teammates. He could not take the game seriously, though at first he tried to conform.

Nobody spots abnormality quicker than youngsters among themselves. Bill was not popular.

"You got a trick," they would say to him.

Bill would not answer. He had no trick. He was merely aware of the complex ballistics of a hurtling object in space. Like a computer, programmed by his amazing eyesight, he knew exactly where his bat would place the ball.

"We're on the same team, aren't we?" they would ask him. "Tell us how you do it."

"How do you?" I asked him at home.

"I tried to tell them," he said, "but it was impossible to communicate." The explanation, which he faithfully related to me, involved trajectories and variable velocities in the Birkhoff-Vallarta flat-space continuum.

"I see," I said, nodding.

He had not of course communicated with me either, nor could I guess where he had picked up the terms.

He looked at me searchingly. I buried my nose in the newspaper.

Bill's excellence, and his attitude, generated hostility among his teammates, for they thought he was a snob or a fake, and even the coach was convinced that somehow he was cheating. Shortly he dropped out and gave up sports altogether.

"The competitions seem pointless," he said to me. "Like attempting to excel in chipping a flint."

I said to him, "Damn it, Bill! Competition builds character!"

He answered, "What kind?"

"A man's!" was on the tip of my tongue, but I never voiced such a sentiment, not to Bill. A conviction had grown in my heart that Bill had formed his own estimate of men and that it was low.

"They didn't want me on the team," he said, shrugging, "and frankly I don't enjoy the game; so I think I'll drop out."

I suppose I looked disappointed.

"I'm sorry, Dad," he said.

"Well, I suppose not everybody's cut out for athletics. But you're good at them, those that require speed and precision, I mean, and it seems a shame, Bill."

"Dad, did you ever smell a locker room after a game?"

"Sure," I said. "Why?"

He looked ashamed, as if somehow he had failed. "It sickens me, physically, like the animal smells in a zoo."

"It's only good healthy sweat," I said.

"I can't help it if it makes me sick."

It was another example of his supersensitivity; or perhaps the odor of humans was animal to him.

"Well," I said, "even if you let athletics go and just concentrate on your studies there's no harm done. That's something you like, anyhow."

One day, thinking to teach him how to use the dictionary, I asked him to look up the spelling of the word "conduit." I had often used this word in the course of my work on The Dam, but this time I had occasion to write it in a report. Bill not only knew the word without referring to the dictionary, but he spelled it correctly for me and gave me its Latin derivation. I looked it up myself then, and discovered that Bill knew the word that came before, which was "conductor," and he knew the word that came after, which was "condyle." Shortly, with an odd sensation at my spine, I discovered that he knew every word in the dictionary. No matter which page I turned to, no matter what word I picked out, he could spell it and give me the meaning.

"That's amazing," I said.

He thought he had pleased me. He smiled his wonderfully appealing smile; it always seemed to light up the room; and, like a child, he seemed to be asking for praise. I was too upset to praise him much, and he seemed to retire into himself. I did not want to talk about it. It was therefore much later that I became aware that he knew every word in every book in the house. More, he knew all the books by heart and understood them.

When no one was looking I would spy on the way he read a book or a newspaper. His eye did not travel from line to line. He "saw" like a camera, instantaneously and, like a camera, he retained every detail. It was never necessary for him to review his lessons in school, for once having read them he recorded them permanently in his brain.

When he began to realize that his manner of reading differed from that of other people he tried to hide his gift. He was wonderfully thoughtful of me. When he would see me covertly watching him he would purposely spend several minutes on a page so as not to appear unusual, till I would look away; and then I would hear again the flip, flip, flipping of the pages as the information torrented into his amazing brain. In this consideration for my feelings he was like an eagle, born to soar but doomed to dwell among stupid chickens, trying to hide the fact that an eagle's nature is to fly and a chicken's to scratch in the dirt.

Still I refused to admit to myself that Bill might be some sort of genius. I had heard of several instances of photographic memory: one was a man who could remember the serial number of every boxcar in a mile-long freight train;

lots of people knew the Bible by heart; and there was the
case of the rabbi who could recite the entire Talmud, all
forty volumes. And there were of course the chess players,
who could remember every move and foresee a hundred more
in advance. I was afraid of the word "freak"; I assured myself
that Bill was not more freakish than these. And even if he
was strangely gifted, freaks were not necessarily bad freaks.
The first double rose, which possesses a sweet fragrance, was
also a mutant or freak, offspring of the odorless and rather
crude wild rose. I pondered the term "wild." How wild,
even savage, I saw myself in contrast to my sensitive son.

"You are certainly the only boy in the world who can remember a whole book just by reading it," I said, when I got
used to the idea and could bring myself to praise him.

"Angélique Bolduc can," he said.

"Like you?"

"Yes. We don't know why everybody can't. So we don't
talk about it except among ourselves."

"Do you like her?"

"She is absolutely lovely!" he said, and he flushed so
normally, so self-consciously, that I heaved a great sigh of
relief. He had begun to like girls. *That* wasn't freakish. I do
not know anything that ever pleased me more.

"She and I usually tie for first place in class."

"Usually?"

"Oh, sometimes I let her win on purpose."

That sounded good too. He was learning the first lesson
a gentleman has to.

"How old is Angélique?"

"Just my age," he said.

That night I spoke to Betty about the incident. It had
always been difficult for her to talk about him except when
he was very young. He had grown away from her early. "He

never seems to need me," she would say. Later she would express herself plaintively, "He doesn't love me. I feel it."

"He is very polite and considerate," I once said, when he was five or six years old.

She had answered, "Since when is a little boy polite and considerate? He ought to be playing in the mud and getting into fights and pulling wings off flies." Later on she seldom spoke of him at all and would only murmur, "He frightens me."

But now I had good news.

"Bill has some mighty peculiar abilities," I said, "but I guess every parent hopes his kids will grow up to be smarter than he was."

"Not as smart as Bill," she said.

"Well, there's nothing peculiar about his attitude towards girls. He's taken a shine to the Bolduc girl, and I expect they'll be going to dances soon, and probably he'll begin swiping my cigarettes and trying to hide the tobacco smell on his breath. Then one day he'll sneak a cocktail. Then he'll be just like everybody else, only just a little smarter. He'll mix with people more, and when he grows up he'll always be sure of a top-notch job."

Betty said, "I hope so."

"Sure he will," I said.

She said, "How well do you actually know Angélique Bolduc?"

"I know the family, of course. A nice ordinary family. She ought to be a nice ordinary girl. She'll do him good."

"She's just like him," Betty said without a smile.

So there were two of them, both born during the glare of The Twenty Minute War. My feeling of elation diminished.

I thought a moment. "He did say she remembers books the way he does," I said.

"I'm not at all surprised, though he never told me that. Probably they hide it."

"Well, hiding's a good sign. I never did like intellectual snobs."

"I wonder what else they hide. I don't feel I know Bill at all."

"Damn it, as long as he likes the girl I don't care how smart he is. He's always liked pets, too. That's pretty normal. I can't remember when we didn't have a dog."

"He doesn't pay much attention to it any more. And I know he can't stand the smell."

"I suppose boys lose interest in their dogs when they discover girls."

"Sometimes I get the impression he thinks of humans as dogs, nice little animals to amuse him and train to do tricks and to be petted and pitied because they're animals."

She spoke bitterly, but in my mind I tried to explain away her attitude by the fact that she had never been able to mother him; we had no other children; he demanded nothing of her; it was probably quite true that he had never needed her. He had seemed, however, to need me.

I now believe he needed me only as a guide book to teach him what he should hide. By observing me he could learn what it is to be ordinary, and not flaunt his superiority. In the end, of course, it was found out; and he died because of it.

It was only natural that Bill should outstrip his schoolmates in study, and for some time I was pleased. A new educational program had been adopted. Owing to the depopulation of great areas of the planet there was an enormous demand for trained scientists, engineers and even professors of the humanities, lest the more abstract aspects of our culture be lost. A series of state examinations, called "quality-centered," scientifically screened the younger generation. Those who could qualify were placed in advanced classes regardless of age. Thus Bill was continually pushed ahead, and graduated from college at the age of sixteen. He was raced through postgraduate work and at eighteen he had a Ph.D. in science.

The papers editorialized, "We have solid reason to be proud of our new academic system. There is now in our colleges and in our Institute for Advanced Studies a considerable body of young men and women who have achieved doctorates at an age when their fathers and mothers were still in high school." There was usually some complacent remark like, "Most educators believe this would always have been possible if youth had been given a chance to realize its potential to the full at all stages of its development instead of being held back by curricula that were relics of the Dark Ages and administered by a hierarchy of intellectual bigots who purposely made learning as difficult and sterile as possible. The Twenty Minute War changed all that." I could never follow these pronouncements, because whichever side I took they put me in the wrong; but they were treated with great respect by all who understood them and hailed as progress.

I, who was the father of one of these callow Ph.D.'s, was not convinced; and I wished Bill were more competitive and less intelligent. I disliked the feeling of inferiority that I experienced whenever Bill came into the room. I loved him deeply, and Betty tried to, but he made us feel ill at ease and there is no doubt that secretly and ashamedly we resented him.

Many people did. I shall never forget his first and only fist fight. It had been late in coming; I had had some lurking fears that he might be a sissy; but when it came I was alarmed at the successful manner in which he handled it.

It happened on graduation night, when he was sixteen and got his first college degree. Bill had taken the Bolduc girl to the graduation dance. I looked at her more critically now, trying to see her through Bill's young eyes; he was certainly right in his estimation of her looks: Angélique was stunningly beautiful, slender, tall, and with deep brown intelligent eyes. I thought I had never seen so perfectly matched a young couple, and they were, as usual, the youngest of the graduating crowd.

They went to a quiet restaurant for a snack after the dance. Neither smoked nor drank.

A noisy crowd of undergraduates, all older than they, were in an adjoining booth, slightly tipsy. One of them, a hulking two-hundred-pounder who was on the wrestling team, became offensive, as Bill described the incident to me, for of course I hurried up to the college at once, fearing Bill might be in serious trouble, since the wrestler was hospitalized for a broken arm.

"What did he say that was offensive?" I asked my son.

"Oh, it wasn't so much what he said. He was drunk and probably didn't know."

"Well, saying offensive things is usually how fights start," I said, remembering back to my own youth when I both gave and received my share.

Bill laughed. "He said what you might expect from a muscular buffoon. He said, 'Baby, I'd sure like to wrestle you.'"

"Oh, he did, eh? Naturally Angélique got sore and so did you. I don't blame you," I said.

He looked at me oddly. "Why in the world should Angélique or I take offense at such a fantastic notion?"

"You mean you didn't?"

He laughed his silvery laugh again. It always reminded me of music.

"We were delighted that he possessed the imagination to entertain such a concept. We felt a certain kinship with the poor lout."

"Well, then, what did he say?"

"He said of course, as such creatures often do, wallowing in their coarseness, 'A good cigarette and a good—' I shan't offend you with a word?"

"I think I know the word."

"He said a cigarette and a good one of those would probably kill me."

"He used *that* dirty word in front of Angélique? No wonder you got sore."

"Not at all. Why shouldn't he use the first word that popped into his animal mind?" Bill asked, again giving me his queer uncomprehending look. "No, that wasn't what offended me."

"It would have me," I said.

"I know, Dad. The caveats of their speech always bewildered me till I learned about them."

"Caveats?" I thought. "*Their* speech? Whose?"

But Bill answered me before I formulated the question. No doubt I had looked perplexed, as indeed I was, and he translated:

"The tabu terms that most people avoid, as if lightning would strike if they employed them; yet all the time they act like swine in heat. That sort of thing made me wonder when I was a child."

It had never made *me* wonder, for it constituted a gentleman's code.

"The thing that offended me," Bill said, looking a little uneasy, "was that the wrestler got up and staggered over to our booth and took his cigarette and tried to thrust it into my mouth. The stench of him was dreadful, and of course I could not have smoked the cigarette. I tried a cigarette once. First it intoxicated me, then it made me violently sick to my stomach."

I smiled. "That's not so unusual the first time."

"Oh, yes it is. They don't ordinarily intoxicate. I went unconscious for over an hour."

"Maybe you're allergic."

"Decidedly. Alcohol is even worse. Angélique is the same way. I tried a sip of whisky once. The effect was something you would not understand."

"Oh, I don't know. I've been drunk a time or two." But any attempt to be hail-fellow-well-met always failed with Bill.

"I'm afraid our metabolism is a little different," he said, as if he did not care to pursue the subject.

"Who's 'our'?" I asked.

"I meant 'mine,'" he said, and went on with what I thought was a touch of commendable young pride. Or perhaps he was talking down to me in terms I could understand. "When this hulking ape thrust the cigarette under my nose I carelessly inhaled a deep breath through my nostrils. It stimulated me strongly and I lost my head. Angélique warned me not to hurt him, but by that time I had twisted his arm till it snapped. Only when I felt his bones break in a compound fracture did I recover my aplomb. Then I quieted his bellowing and took him to a hospital."

"You'd better be careful when he gets out. He'll wring your neck. You've made a lasting enemy."

"Oh, I don't know," he said, smiling. "Would you like to see him?"

"No, I don't think you need any help. How did you quiet him?"

"Oh, I just talked to him."

"Just like that?"

"It wasn't difficult."

"How did you break his arm? Judo?"

"Something like that. It's in lots of Japanese books."

"I suppose so," I said, rather unhappily; for now I knew that Bill, among his other accomplishments, could also read Japanese.

I did see the wrestler, however, when he was discharged from the hospital. He made a special point of coming around to apologize to Betty and me for his ungentlemanly behavior. He was obviously the bully type and his desire to apologize seemed quite out of character, till suddenly I detected in his speech, which was otherwise somewhat slangy, a precise little insert that he delivered in a changed voice; it was almost as if Bill were dictating it: "I am extremely regretful for my wicked misconduct, committed against Mr. Young," he said, "most grossly and through my own stupidity and inadequacy; and I promise to amend my conduct and never again in thought or deed offend him or anyone like him. This I will never forget."

"That's very handsome of you," I said. "I'm sure there's no harm done. I'm glad you don't carry a grudge. I know Bill doesn't."

"Mr. Young is the most wonderful person in the world," he said with a look like a dog adoring its master.

"We'll drink a toast to that," I said, pouring him a nip.

He watched me down mine, raised his own and set it untasted on the table.

"I've lost my taste for the stuff," he said. "I used to love it, or a big beer, after a match, to celebrate. Never in training, of course. Now I can't touch it. Damned funny."

Betty said when he was gone, "He talked just like any good-natured young man till he got to that stilted speech of apology. Then he talked like somebody else."

"I felt that too," I said, troubled.

I was troubled by more than his speech. As I reconstructed the physical setting in the restaurant, Bill and Angélique in a booth, the wrestler hovering over them, probably leaning against the table and blocking the way, *how* had Bill managed to move so swiftly out of his seat and get behind the larger man and twist his arm? In the placement of the opponents the odds were all in favor of the wrestler.

But I was so relieved that there would be no reprisal for the incident that I forgot to ask Bill and the wrestler left before I thought of it again. No doubt it was owing to Bill's amazing ability to move fast when he wanted to, like the precision with which he had pitched and batted and raced round the diamond when he used to play baseball.

"I don't see why the man came to apologize at all," I said.

Betty said, "I don't suppose you'd care to hear what I think."

"I don't know why not," I said.

"Well, you'll never hear a word against Bill."

"There is nothing against him that I know of."

"Well, I think Bill hypnotized him and gave him a post-hypnotic suggestion about not liking liquor."

"Do you actually think Bill can hypnotize people?" I asked.

"He can do pretty nearly everything else," she said, frowning, frightened as always.

I had always denied that hypnotism existed, because I didn't understand it, and things I don't understand I usually claim aren't real. Then I learned that hypnotism did exist, and so I thought about it as little as possible.

"Well, if he did hypnotize him," I said, "he only made a friend out of him and taught him not to drink. There's nothing wrong in that. And hypnotism isn't supernatural, whatever else it may be. So neither is Bill. He's certainly different, but he's not an angel and he's not a devil; so he isn't supernatural."

"He's supernormal, though," Betty said.

"Well, so are all geniuses," I said.

I was willing by now to concede that Bill was a genius, and "genius" is a better word about a son than "freak."

Betty added, tight-lipped, "That wrestler acted brainwashed."

That made me chuckle. I had never believed in that nonsense either. True, there were weird cases of queer confessions a generation ago, where witnesses testified against themselves in traitor trials, but I had always been satisfied with the well-documented explanations that they were crackpots to begin with or that they had been starved or drugged or tortured or that they were trying to protect families or loved ones from reprisals. And the process took months. Bill could not have brainwashed the wrestler in a couple of hours. I was quite willing to believe that the human heart could be worked on to make a man admit anything to protect someone else; but I would never concede that a human brain could be destroyed by anything but physical means. That a stronger mind, be it quicker, finer, better informed or even the mind of a genius of vast and abnormal capacity could permanently alter it, could render it flabby and submissive, or even enslave it, I stoutly refused to believe; nor could I imagine anything so reprehensible.

I have now changed this view.

CHAPTER 3

DURING the college and postgraduate years of one's children I suppose it is inevitable that a parent loses touch with them. It certainly is not the same as when they lived at home, and when they finish their schooling it is natural that, to a degree, they are strangers. But when Bill told me that a prominent engineering firm had hired him the day he got his Ph.D. I thought him more distant than a son ought to be. I congratulated him heartily on his position, which proved to be one of great trust. He took it all rather coolly.

"It will take every minute of your working hours, every ounce of your energy to make good," I said, "but I know you will. God bless you."

"It doesn't seem *too* formidable," he said, and I thought I heard scorn in his voice. But perhaps it was only confidence. Perhaps, I thought, it merely reflected the spirit of confidence that animated the whole world. I, who could remember the Second World War and The Twenty Minute War, often contrasted our present time of peace and security with the earlier days when men dwelt in fear of a vast explosion of death and destruction brought on by the jealousies and conflicting ideologies of sovereign national states. All that had come and gone. Mankind and the earth had survived it. The world had learned its lesson. Never, scholars told us, had there been such a period of serenity, joy, tolerance, health, prosperity and enthusiasm. The devastated world needed to be rebuilt and was rapidly rebuilding. So much had been destroyed that everything was new. Nothing had to be patched up because everything had to be replaced and replacement is always better.

Occasionally, here and there around the world, there could be observed traces of the old nationalisms; but these were promptly put down. Another war was unthinkable. National war was equated by the new World Law with individual murder, and there were means at hand to punish it as such. The world had at last become truly One World. No one grew sentimental over this or took credit for it: it was simply One World or none; and the instinct to survive, now codified and elevated into World Law, was recognized as the strongest impulse in the nature of man, and rightfully so.

Some said we would stagnate. Some said so secure a life would be nothing but a bore. They did not reckon with all the great challenges that faced us in the rebuilding of the physical destruction that had occurred. And when that would be accomplished, there would lie before us, to fire the imagination and appeal to the adventurous, the conquest of space and the mysteries of the stars, and the means were at hand to explore them. Surely the era was glamorous and inviting.

Many remembered the fifteenth century and the voyages of Columbus and the burst of civilizing activity that followed for hundreds of years. Ours too was an age of daring, of adventure, of bold new ideas and the flowering of immeasurable happiness, soundly based on the realization that war would

never happen again and man had finally reached the stature
for which he had been created. Man at last was at peace
with himself and lord of the beckoning universe. Or so I
thought, like almost everybody else. A select and puzzled
few knew better, but kept their knowledge to themselves.

On one of those beautiful evenings that still are with us,
about sunset time when the sky blazed with the gorgeous
colors that we are told will last for centuries, Bill unexpectedly showed up with Angélique Bolduc to tell us he had
a new job. They looked like angels. Angélique's beauty had
always been breath-taking; it seemed now to approach the
ethereal. I have already described my boy. In my admiration for their physical good looks and the mental compati-
bility I knew they enjoyed I could not but think what a
good thing it would be if they married. Of course, they never
did, and I seriously doubt whether marriage, as we know it,
ever entered their strange and bewildering minds.

"What is the nature of your new work?" I asked. I assumed it was some sort of engineering, since that was what
he was trained in; but I had long since stopped asking him
details because he would grow impatient at my inability to
understand his intricate technical vocabulary. If he had
stuck to one language I might have plodded along, but he
would use German, French and other foreign terms if they
were more descriptive or accurate, and he would introduce
the most obscure mathematical formulas into an answer to
the simplest question of mine. I do not think he was being
an intellectual snob; I think he was truly trying to answer
my questions. Later he gave up the attempt, since he saw
I could never keep up with his speed of thought. The saddest
part of his abandoning his earlier willingness to educate me
was his acceptance of the fact that we were too far apart to
make the effort worth while. I would never catch up; it was

like Einstein trying to teach the multiplication tables to a backward child—but like Einstein, he was tolerant and kind once he realized the utter impossibility of establishing communication. So he talked to me in a manner that must have been baby talk for him.

"The work involves navigation, Dad, just as yours always has, but not at sea." I assumed he might mean aircraft for the new project for manned missiles to the moon. Interest in travel to the moon and the establishment of an astronomical observatory there had revived of late, after long being held in abeyance by reason of the vast reconstruction projects required here on our home planet, which we had so vilely abused. But his job aimed higher than the moon.

His work, he said, would take him to the Kamchatka Peninsula, where an experimental base would be built to explore the planets.

"We know practically everything about the moon," he said, observing my blank face, "but we know very little about the planets, and it's just as easy to get to them as to the moon and we'll learn a lot more when we do."

Betty and I, though we should have known better, held to the old prejudices that thought of places like Kamchatka as vastly far away, hazardous to get to and impossible to live in.

"How long is the trip to Kamchatka, Bill?" I said.

From The Dam to Kamchatka was 153 minutes, he said. "I am to be stationed there."

"You can get home for Sunday dinners!" I said.

"Why yes," he said, as if the idea were totally new to him. "I suppose I could."

Betty sighed, and I saw in her face that she had realized before I did that he had no desire nor had he made any plans ever to come home again. After twenty-one years of marriage a husband can often tell what a wife is thinking without her ever saying a word because they have grown so close to each other. I knew she was hurt and angry. Here again Bill did not need her, or even plan to see her again, his own mother!

But he too sensed that she was piqued. And he, who had to learn the simple things, but never twice, said with a charming smile, "I'll come home every chance I get, Mother. The first month or so may be pretty busy and keep me on the job."

"Who's the senior commander there?" I asked. "Maybe I know him if he's a Navy man."

It was somebody named Johnson or Fairfax, I don't know. I forgot it. The name meant nothing to me.

"He's a new officer in the Space Administration," Bill said. "One of us."

"One of whom?"

"I mean he's quite young and I doubt if you've ever heard of him."

"How old is he?"

"Twenty," said Bill, who was also twenty, as was Angélique.

At this Betty went to the kitchen to prepare dinner.

"This commander of yours," I said, "must have quite a staff. I've seen the maps of Kamchatka. It's a pretty mountainous place."

"We'll level what we need to. There are ten of us working on it. The heavy work will be done by a few hundred bright helots."

Angélique shot him a warning glance.

"Construction engineers," he said, correcting himself. I had caught him off guard. He had chanced on a term that The Intruders used among themselves. But I remembered the word and I looked it up later and I found that it meant serfs or slaves, a very low class of person considered sub-human and despicable by the aristocrats of ancient Greece. No one ever thought it reprehensible, for example, if a young Spartan warrior, wishing to test a new sword, tested it on a helot at high noon in the main street, leaving the murdered body to be disposed of by a street cleaner, who would also be a helot. This situation was brought about by the fact that the helots were the original natives of Sparta and did not possess the superior qualities of the race that conquered and replaced them.

Though I did not understand the term when Bill first uttered it I did not like his tone, and I said, "I wonder if I'd be bright enough to qualify as one of these helots."

He looked at me sadly. "The hours are long; you are better off here; it would be unwise of you to step out of your profession. I do not believe I'd permit it."

I flared up at him. "Who are you to *permit* your own father to do anything?"

He sighed, then he patted my shoulder. "We're taking only younger men," he said. "There's an age limit and I'm afraid you've passed the critical line."

"Well, I must say, you're logical if nothing else," I said petulantly. I did not like his logic. It was too cold, too in-human. "Did The Big Ice put ice water in your veins instead of good warm human blood? Logic be damned!"

At this point I sustained an eerie impression that Bill and Angélique were communicating with each other. Angélique was saying, "Quiet him." Bill was answering, "No, I just can't do it to my own father. You do it."

I do not mean that they were communicating by telepathy or thought waves or any such nonsense. I had had difficulty believing in hynotism despite all the proofs. As for some weird extrasensory perception, it is believed by the experts not to exist, even among The Intruders. Sensible people who aren't experts knew that all the time. No, it was merely the instantaneous awareness, greatly refined, of the thoughts and emotions that people who know each other very well and are much alike share with each other. I had known, for example, merely by the look on Betty's face that she was leaving the room because Bill had stated that the commanding officer at the Kamchatka Base was twenty years old, and "twenty" struck her as ominously as it did me, since it was just his age and the age of Angélique.

So now there were three of them. And maybe the ten others whom he had mentioned as being in positions of authority on the staff.

The queer "conversation" between Bill and Angélique lasted less than a second, and without greater pause Angélique began to speak.

She drew me away from the subject and calmed me down like a missionary appeasing the wrath of an aborigine. She made me ashamed of the insulting remark about ice water in Bill's veins. Probing my innermost thoughts and sensing exactly what I wanted to hear, she made me feel humble and proud that I was Bill's father. She spoke softly, as Bill always did, with a singular sweetness much like his except that hers was a woman's voice and hence more charming. I remember very little of what she said; I was only aware of her melodious voice and her luminous brown eyes looking intently into mine, full of truth and beauty, filling me with blind trust and evoking in me a desire for unquestioning obedience that I might be worthy of her approval. I do recall, however, that she made excellent sense, and part of the consolation that filled me was based on a flood of biological data—I'm sure that's what it was; it was what I wanted to hear—to the effect that Bill's blood was exactly like mine in pressure, type and chemical content. I believed everything she said. I still do, though I know now how utterly she was subjecting me to her will, and I know that I should have believed her even if she had been lying. I would have had no choice.

Now that Angélique too is dead, and I know more about her and Bill, I wonder if they would have disposed of the Kamchatka helots if the helots had become ill or inefficient or exhausted by their labors, much as we dispose of worn-out beasts of burden and sick pets, and replace them. There were so many replacements available. I greatly fear they might have, for we had done the same thing: Where is Neanderthal Man? Where are the Tasmanians?

As I took Angélique and Bill into the dining room where Betty had set out the dinner it seemed to me that Betty looked at me with something akin to fear in her face and she whispered to me, "Thank God you're all right. I heard her talking. I was afraid she was doing what Bill did to the wrestler."

"What nonsense!" I said, laughing. "Bill, your mother thinks I'm going to give up my smoking and my cocktail before dinner."

They both laughed, and Angélique said, "That would be a pity."

To put Betty at her ease, and also, I confess it, to assure myself that Angélique had not been trying some sneaky trick on my brain, I lit a cigarette and mixed up a shakerful of cocktails. The cigarette tasted better than any I ever had smoked in my life. I raised my eyebrows at Betty as much as to say, "You see, my dear, the young lady has done nothing to me." Betty understood and smiled and we all sat down.

I had taken a great fancy to Angélique. I knew I could trust her; my faith in her understanding and friendship passed all bounds; I knew she would not mind a little joke at Bill's expense.

"He doesn't like these things," I said, indicating the cigarette. "I'll blow it away from him."

"Not at her," Bill said, in his curious tone of command.

"Good Lord, no," I said. I felt I had made a serious social blunder, and stubbed it out and changed the subject.

"Bill may have told you," I said to Angélique, "that he's got a new job up in Kamchatka. To my generation, of course, that sounds very far away, but he tells me it's only a couple of hours. We'll be seeing him often, you will too, I dare say; and we're both very glad."

"Oh, I'm going too," she said. "On the same ship with the others."

"Dr. Bolduc," he said, grinning at her title, which I had not heard before, "is going to do a research paper on the probable cause of the Arctic Hysteria prevalent among the Koryak primitives of Kamchatka."

"But they're all dead," I said. Everyone knew that this unfortunate isolated race had been wiped out by The Big Ice.

"Some of the corpses will have been preserved below frost level," Angélique said very calmly. "It's only a matter of digging them up and doing a neurological dissection and analysis. Arctic Hysteria has always fascinated me."

This conversation was taking place at the dinner table.

"Angélique is an anthropologist," Bill said.

"She's an anthropologist," I said to Betty, who was looking at her with disapproval.

"Mother isn't a scientist," Bill said for our benefit, very kindly, though I think he had already warned Angélique not to pursue the conversation. "She couldn't even cut up a Koryak to see what made it tick."

"I'm so very sorry I talked shop, Mrs. Young," Angélique said, smiling charmingly, leveling her beautiful eyes at her. "It's just that the periodic aberrations of this tribe intrigue me and require explanation."

Betty looked down to avoid her glance and picked at her untouched dinner.

"Doctors are always talking shop," I said jovially, and preened myself on the brilliant glance of thanks I got from Angélique. I felt I had been taken into an inner circle.

"Will there be only men on the plane, Angélique?" Betty asked.

Angélique looked surprised. "Good heavens, I never inquired, Mrs. Young. Do you know, Bill?"

"Only men," Bill said. "Why, Mother?" He too looked surprised.

"Oh, I was only wondering. Only men at the Base too? If you know?"

Both Bill and Angélique shrugged. They hadn't the slightest idea, obviously had never asked.

"Things are different now, Mother," I said. "Every new generation's different from their elders. We were too. Remember?"

"I suppose so," she said.

"Anyhow, they're scientists."

"I just can't help feeling that an attractive girl like you ought not to be the only single woman in a rough mining camp at the end of nowhere among hundreds of men," Betty said. "It's—it's—it's just not right."

Bill and Angélique looked at each other with instant understanding. There followed a moment of colloquy that sounded as if it were out of a first-year book in a foreign-language course.

"I have asked Angélique's hand in marriage and she has done me the honor to accept me," Bill said.

Angélique said, "We are devoted to each other and I shall be proud of my status of wife and the protection of a husband, to whom I will cleave till death us do part."

It was kind of them to improvise this little exchange to put Betty at her ease. There is no cruelty in The Intruders. They are too coldly logical for that. But there is a gulf between our minds and theirs, and, on their part, some disgust. I know now that they equate the holy state of matrimony with tribal scars and Chinese foot binding.

The dinner livened considerably after that. "Well, kids," I said, "this calls for a drink. Betty, we've been giving an engagement party and we didn't even know it! The speed things go at nowadays!"

"Don't they," Betty said, not very pleasantly. She had never been close to Bill. I could see she had taken an instinctive dislike to Angélique. I know now that she was not alone in this aversion, but I, thick-headed as I was and under the spell of my son's charming fiancée, reproached her.

"My dear," I said, "it isn't as if there were any reason why they *have* to get married, which is what you infer. They have made up their own minds about each other, and I, for one, say God bless them."

"I'm sure they have," Betty said.

I was uncomfortable, but Bill and Angélique looked at us with intense interest, like a couple of earnest Jesuits learning Swahili.

Out of politeness they each accepted the highball I made them after dinner. This was a gesture of bravado on my part, for I knew they never touched alcohol; but I felt it important to assert my authority in my own house. Also, I confess, I wanted to assure myself that Angélique had not permanently warped my mind against a harmless and most enjoyable habit. She had not. No drink ever tasted better. I felt at that time great contempt for the weak-minded wrestler. "Muscles in his head too," was the thought that occurred to me.

Bill and Angélique barely touched their lips to the rim of their glasses, and Bill looked at his watch and said they would have to be going now or else miss the plane.

At the door Betty said to Bill, "You haven't told us much about your plans. Your father and I don't even know the date of your wedding. We'd like to give you a nice one."

I admired her restraint, and I could see how hurt she was at their casualness.

"Oh, the wedding. Of course," Angélique said, looking at Bill.

"I expect the Base Commander will take care of that," Bill said.

"Didn't you say he was one of your twenty-year-olds?" Betty said. "Is he also a minister?"

Angélique smiled at her approvingly, detecting the trap. The Intruders admire quick-thinking minds like Betty's.

"There isn't any regular chaplain at the Base, Mrs. Young; but the Base Commander can perform a civil ceremony."

"Like a captain on a ship," Bill said, translating into my terms, smiling at me.

That was true, I said, nodding agreement. True, solid and traditional. What could be more natural than that a new base like Kamchatka would have no churches or chapels yet. I was deeply convinced that Bill and Angélique had made much the best arrangements. They could be trusted in everything. I made some fatuous remark about the grandchildren Betty and I would probably have, starting in nine months unless *that* were speeded up nowadays like everything else.

"We really don't know," Angélique said wistfully. "Truly we don't."

"Nobody knows," Bill said.

These were the last words we ever heard him utter. What overtones they now take on.

Betty said when they were gone, "Her expression when she condescended to mention a baby was the only human look I ever saw on her face." She sighed and continued, "I'd like to have given them a nice wedding. Even Angélique."

I lighted a cigar and leaned back in my chair with Bill's untasted drink. "He never touched it," I said.

"Neither of them did."

"Well, they went through the motions of being polite anyhow," I said.

I seldom get drowsy after dinner, but this night I was utterly at peace with the world. I felt as if everything would always take care of itself and always for the best, and nothing would ever be demanded of me again. I would never be forced to make a decision. I would never be faced with a crisis. I would not even have to think any more. All responsibility would be lifted from me. A feeling of trust and total surrender took hold of me. I felt deliciously drained. I had never experienced anything like it. It was Nirvana. I felt myself drifting off to sleep, and over me, dreamlike, floated and shone the smiling faces of Bill and Angélique, and I seemed to be hearing them say in their beautiful musical voices, "Rest, and leave everything to us."

Betty says that I snoozed about an hour, vacant-faced and smiling like a baby. My cigar went out and she took it from my hand and put it in the ash tray for fear it would fall on the carpet.

Then abruptly I came awake. Betty says I cursed and

shouted, "That damned witch will never set foot in my house again! And she won't marry Bill. I'm still his father!"

My mood had undergone a complete turn-about. I was furious at Angélique and intensely irked with Bill. I was also angry at myself. I had acted like a jellyfish. I had let her bend me utterly to her will. All the resentment I ever had harbored against Bill, his oddities and quirks and above all his inexplicable excellence, flared up double because of Angélique.

His drink was still at my elbow. I tossed it down, wishing I had made it stronger. I had made it weak out of deference to his weakness. It tasted grand. I was not like the wrestler, I thought, exulting. That grappling moron, that savage hulk, that flabby defenseless mind.

I do not defend these unworthy thoughts. I write them because I experienced them at the time, a time which the experts have deemed significant, namely, nine-fifteen that evening.

Just then the telephone rang.

It was very bad news.

CHAPTER 4

BETTY rose to answer the phone. I felt like barking at somebody. I growled, "I'll take it," and reached for the instrument.

"Yes?" I said belligerently.

A cool official voice said, "I should like to speak to Commander Young."

"This is Commander Young."

"So I see," said the voice. "It is good of you to identify
yourself right at the outset. We always need that. It simplifies
things."

"What do you mean, 'So I see'?" I demanded. Betty and I
had never been able to afford one of the new TV telephones,
nor did I see any necessity for them. They are all very well
for families with daughters who talk interminably with their
boy friends, but Betty and I had no need of such a luxury.

"You are in the visual field of the portable transmitter at
your window," the voice said. "You will understand that we
have to have a taped record. This call is made for the purpose
of warning you and your wife to offer no resistance to the
officers at your door. The back door, too, Commander."

"Who the hell are you?" I shouted.

"I am the Commissioner of Police."

I was not in the least alarmed. For years the police had, in the absence of crime, been reduced to the lowest status of municipal functionaries, with little to do but search for lost dogs and direct traffic.

"What do you want with me?"

"I should like to talk to you about the accident in which your son, Wilson Young, Jr., and the girl Angélique Bolduc, were involved."

"Accident? When? What's happened?"

"A traffic accident, Commander, at nine-fifteen this evening. They were both killed."

Within the hour I was to learn that my behavior on receiving this news, which was delivered with calculated cruelty and cunning, predetermined in its suddenness, did much to exonerate me from the suspicion that usually attaches to parents of Intruders. I am told that my reactions, permanently taped and simultaneously transmitted visually to the Commissioner's office, revealed nothing of interest. I emitted an audible groan. I said, "My God, no!" I hung up the telephone, missing the cradle, and fumbled it into place. I sat down in a chair. When Betty rushed over and said, "What is it?" I said, "There's been an accident to Bill. Bill and Angélique. They say it's serious."

"They're dead," she said.

"Maybe it's not true," I said, putting my arm around her.

At this point the front door opened, though it had an automatic spring lock; and two policemen entered and said, "Please come with us, Commander. You too, Mrs. Young."

We knew they were policemen because they were armed, the only persons on the planet who are.

They refused to answer questions and there was silence in the darkened car while we were driven to the police station, a small inoffensive building with nothing to identify it except the seal of the World Chiefs over the door. Betty wept softly on my shoulder. I glowered and comforted her, muttering, "Maybe it's not true. Maybe they made a mistake. Maybe it's somebody else."

"No," she whispered, "I know they're dead. You were yourself again the very moment they ceased to exist. It is for the best."

I thought she was hysterical. Now I know she was right. This is also the opinion of the experts, who observed and listened to us all the way to the station. The police car was equipped with hidden UV and IF TV transmitters and every word we whispered, every expression on our faces, is now a permanent part of the dossier on Bill and Angélique. It was my first introduction to the still-continuing war against The Intruders. And I had thought the police were nothing but dog catchers!

We did not stop at the front door of the police station but drove around to the rear. This was an ambulance entrance, little used because its only function was to give temporary surgery to victims of serious traffic accidents before they were sent to a hospital. Fortunately there are very few of them nowadays.

We were met by a young doctor in a white surgical coat and a stupid face. He had an insufferably officious manner. I hated him on sight.

"Commander and Mrs. Young?"

"Yes," I said.

"I am instructed to ask you to identify the body. Kindly follow me."

Betty clung to me. "I knew it was true," she said.

He led us down a white corridor into a white cold room. I should judge that the temperature was about fifty degrees.

There was an antiseptic odor. On a marble slab with a bloody sheet over him in the center of the room lay my boy. How bereft of all dignity, how helpless, how small is the dead body from which the human soul has flown!

"This way, Commander," said the doctor.

I went toward the marble slab with a feeling in my heart like one who approaches a marble altar on which lies all that is left of the sacrifice. "They have slain him," I am said to have muttered. This remark was much questioned, but forgiven me later. The doctor lifted the sheet and asked me, "Is this the body of your son, Wilson Young, Jr.?" The query struck me as unnecessarily formal and legalistic under the trying circumstances. It was, of course, for the dossier.

"Yes," I said without hesitation, for despite the wounds there was no doubt that it was Bill.

Betty had remained in the background, but now she too was summoned forward.

"Is that necessary?" I said. "I have identified him."

"We need both parents' identification," he said.

I took her arm, fearful that she might faint; but she walked steadily enough.

"Is this the body of your son, Wilson Young, Jr.?" said the doctor again, repeating the same formula. I had clenched my fist and I was tempted to smash the inquisitor straight in his square blue jaw, but by now I suspected we were observed and I said, "Maybe it's his job, dear."

"Yes, that's Bill," she said. She averted her eyes and sobbed.

"The Commissioner wants to see you," the doctor said. "You will kindly follow me." It seemed to me his voice had lost some of its icy hate. "I am very sorry for you."

"Where is the girl?" Betty said.

"Her father, a Narcisse Bolduc, is attempting to make the identification. It is rather more difficult in her case."

I could feel Betty shudder as she leaned on me.

The doctor ushered us into the paneled office of the Commissioner, who stared at us suspiciously for a moment, then motioned us into chairs with a grim nod.

"Parents of the male?" he asked the doctor, without greeting us.

"Yes, sir. Commander and Mrs. Young."

"Well, Doctor?" the Commissioner said, looking at Betty and me.

The doctor smiled and shook his head. "No, sir. Quite ordinary."

"Not one of them, eh?"

"Not a chance."

"Too old, I suppose. That's been the record."

"That, of course. But they don't fit the pattern either."

"I hope I never get an old one."

"So far they've all been twenty years old," the doctor said. "One over twenty would require total revision of our working hypothesis. We'd have to start from scratch, screen everybody."

"Let's pray we never catch one."

"Pray is about all we can do, sir. But we don't think we will. We're pretty sure it was the War that did it."

The Commissioner of Police now condescended to recognize our presence. He exhaled a great sigh of relief and turned toward Betty and me with a look of understanding on his face and said, "I am terribly sorry about the accident. Permit me to extend my deep sympathy to you and Mrs. Young."

"How did it happen?" I said.

"He was driving toward the airport with Dr. Angélique Bolduc," the Commissioner began.

"Yes, we know that. He told us that. They were going to be married and work at the Kamchatka Base."

"Yes. They had got about a mile from your house when he lost control of the car and collided with a police car."

"I've never seen a police car. Not for years, at any rate," I said.

"They aren't marked, you know. The nature of our work is confidential. The accident seemed not to be serious; both cars were traveling at a reasonable rate of speed; they simply locked bumpers. But a crowd of curiosity seekers gathered. There are so few traffic accidents nowadays with the automatic controls; it is natural for a crowd to gather when a freak one occurs; you remember the old days, how accidents always used to draw crowds?"

The doctor interrupted, "It won't do, Commissioner. They can take the truth."

"Yes, I remember the crowds," I said.

The Commissioner went on, hoping to spare us, "Unfortunately, your son had been drinking. He staggered out of the car and began to berate the plainclothesman with whom he had collided. He became quite offensive."

"He hadn't had a drop to drink," I said. "I offered him a highball, but he didn't touch it."

"Analysis of his blood showed a concentration of alcohol well above the level to induce irresponsible intoxication," the doctor said.

"It isn't true!" I cried.

"It is already in the record," he answered.

"You were mighty quick to put the blame on him," I said.

"Oh, the girl was drunk, too. That is also in the record," the doctor said.

"There was a scuffle, and the crowd took the part of the policeman," the Commissioner said.

"I'd like to talk to that damned policeman," I said.

"I'm afraid you can't. Your son killed him with a single blow in the solar plexus. Nobody actually saw the blow. They move very fast, these people, but they know exactly where to strike. The poor officer never caught his breath; he died of suffocation. Then the crowd closed in."

"It's all in the record," the doctor said.

It was too pat. I thought of Bill's wounds. "I don't believe a word of this!" I cried.

"Would you care to see the tapes?" the Commissioner said.

I glared at him.

"What tapes?"

"He and the Bolduc girl have been under surveillance for some time, along with others," the Commissioner said. "The record is full and significant, beginning with the time when they were detected by an agent whose suspicions were aroused when he overheard them speaking together in a foreign language."

"Lots of people do that," I said.

"This was Sanskrit," the doctor said. "An Indian pundit identified it."

"Bill must have got hold of another foreign book," I said sighing. "He could read books faster than I can read a page."

"They all can," the doctor said. "We believe he taught it to the girl, probably in five minutes or so, and they used it for a sort of pig Latin when they wanted to converse privately."

"They didn't need pig Latin for that," I said. "All they had to do was look at each other."

The Commissioner raised his eyebrows. "Ah, you know about that? You are more cooperative than most of their parents, Commander. I think I can safely show you the tapes."

Betty shook her head. "I don't think I'd care to see them. It was really an execution, wasn't it, Commissioner?"

"The record will list it as a traffic accident," the Commissioner said sternly. "Anything else would be most dangerous, for all of us."

"I'd like to go home," Betty said. She was pale and drawn.

"We can put you up here," the Commissioner said. "You deserve a good night's rest."

"Not here," Betty said. "Not where they are."

"At least take one of these before you go to bed tonight, both of you," the doctor said, giving us each one small white pill in a little white envelope. He smiled in a friendly fashion. "I know this has been a trial for you."

I hesitated, but Betty said, "Thank you, Doctor," and took the envelopes.

"I shall want to see you again tomorrow," the Commissioner said.

"No doubt your men will call for us," I said sarcastically. There was still venom in me.

"Why, of course they will," Betty said, with a bite in her tone that I recognized. "You and I are very important people."

"Yes, you are," the doctor said.

When we were at home I said, "Betty, don't let's take those pills. They might be poison."

She laughed bitterly. "If they were going to execute us too, we'd be dead already. Do you hear that, Commissioner? Am I right, Doctor?" She addressed the question to the blank walls of our bedroom.

"Yes, I suppose we're still under surveillance," I said, lowering my voice.

"Do you really believe that they can't hear us?" she said. "Speak right up and ask the wall how they're getting along with chopping him up and counting his corpuscles. You know what they're doing, don't you?"

"Yes, I suppose they'd have to perform a thorough autopsy on a man like Bill," I said.

"Not a man, a creature!" she sobbed. "Oh my strange, my beautiful, my distant, my darling boy! Oh Bill, how I loved, how I feared our child!"

She had not called me "Bill" for a very long time. Bill, Jr. had pre-empted the name.

"Come, come," I said, with a brave attempt to be comforting. "We'd better swallow those pills."

They were quite harmless apparently. At any rate we survived a dreamless, refreshing night. Next morning we were again conducted to the presence of the Commissioner and the doctor. Both were sober faced, and we four were alone in the paneled office, though what electronic eyes and ears were trained on us I can only conjecture.

"I hope you had a pleasant rest," the Commissioner said.

"I think you already know," I said.

"Of course I do, Commander. I can also answer Mrs. Young's penetrating query about the autopsy, which has now been perfomed. It turned out very much like what we expected."

"I heard nothing on the news about the accident," Betty said.

The Commissioner shook his head. "You won't."

"Nor the death of the policeman," she said.

"No, we won't make that public either. There has been too much publicity already. In the war for survival in which we are engaged we would lose if the enemy were to discover that we know he exists and have means of recognizing him."

"Then it was an execution," Betty said. Betty is always quicker to grasp the essential than I am. I suppose it is woman's intuition.

"Yes, Mrs. Young, it was an execution. One of many."

"And the crowd who stomped and slashed them to death? They were your men?" I asked.

"Yes, Commander, they were my men. Men like you and me."

"They needn't have been so vicious," I said.

Bill had been wickedly beaten. Long after he must have been dead, they still kicked and pummelled and bashed. Angélique, I learned, fared even worse. Narcisse Bolduc had difficulty identifying her. Her frail and slender body was absolutely shredded and most obscenely insulted. Even in death, it would seem, the instinct to kill did not stop; and the killers seemed to demonstrate by the manner of their slashing that the thing they feared most was that beings like Angélique and Bill would reproduce and nurse their own superior kind.

"It is not easy to control the dedicated men who carry out these executions," the Commissioner said. "They have seen what The Intruders are capable of. One of my better agents went to a wrestling match some time ago and heard someone behind him remark, 'This is the factor in their biology that gave rise to The Twenty Minute War.' It seemed like a harmless remark at the time, one any sensitive youngster might make. But later the wrestler was retired from the ring, and later still he was found wandering the streets quite brainless. He is now in an institution with others of their victims. Then the agent remembered that the person behind him had also said, 'Ultimately we shall have to eliminate them,' and reported the incident. There have been others, seemingly innocuous but filled with potential danger. We investigate every one, and a suspect is placed under surveillance. We are often successful, and an enemy is eliminated. Sometimes we are not. I confess that we never did find The Intruder who blasted the brain of the wrestler."

I looked at Betty, who looked at me.

"We do not know how they propose to exterminate us," the Commissioner continued. "So far we know nothing of their life span or the age at which they will achieve maturity or whether they already have. They may be very short-lived, like fruit flies. On the other hand, the age of twenty may be, for them, kindergarten."

"We had often wondered how long Bill would live," Betty said. "We know now."

"If children in kindergarten can do what they can, supposing the worst, namely, that their life span is two or three times ours," the Commissioner said, "think what they will be capable of at their maturity."

"It no longer concerns Betty and me," I said.

"It does," the Commissioner said, "though you and your wife cannot understand so at the moment. It must never be forgotten that The Intruders hate us."

But I knew they did not, not Bill, not Angélique. It was the Commissioner and men like him, even me, I'm afraid, who hated, at least who feared them. Poor children! Poor innocent superchildren! Yet they share our humanity. We produced them. We are responsible for their existence, and our follies are responsible for their oddities. If we perish at their hands, if they exterminate us because we are too backward, too savage to live, it will be our own fault. So far, through their immaturity, unaware of their own powers, if they are really long-lived, or through their innate gentleness, to which I am witness, they have shown tolerance. But so did we towards the Tasmanians, until, exasperated, we obliterated them.

In our sorrow Betty and I must have presented the very picture of dejection. The blue-chinned doctor said kindly to me, "I'm sorry, Commander. It is not your fault that you sired a mutant, nor is it your wife's." It was small comfort.

He told us what was wrong with our boy, and with Angélique, and with all The Intruders. I got the impression that he was sorry not that they were dead, in fact he seemed quite glad, but that Betty and I were Bill's parents and would be under certain restrictions from then on. He was very patient, assuming that we would not understand. Fortunately I have a mind for figures, and the mathematics involved were quite simple—frightening but simple.

Here follow the doctor's words. It must be borne in mind that he is a scientist, dedicated to the extermination of The Intruders, nearly as cool and logical as they are. This is what he said:

"I must tell you, Commander, that an autopsy on your son is completed. It is only partially complete in the case of the girl because her head was badly crushed, but we are pretty sure about her too. Exactly the same as Bill. Bill possessed a brain with a surface area—that is the area which thinks—of 4800 square centimeters. Mine is 2400. Just half. So is yours. So is your wife's. So is every other human being's except in the case of The Intruders—if indeed they are human. Theirs is 4800. Exactly twice as much."

I was aware now where the explanation would lead. Here was the scientific answer to Bill's amazing reading powers, his photographic memory and all the other strange futuristic aspects of his personality. But nothing the doctor was to tell me was to explain his nobility.

I said, wondering why I was championing the dead, except that I could not help it, "Bill wasn't a freak. His head perhaps was somewhat large but it wasn't deformed or bulbous like the 'attractions' I used to see in sideshows at county fairs. They were mostly poor demented folk."

The doctor said, "You must think of the brain not in terms of cubic capacity as if it were a tank, but in terms of a flat surface like one of your nautical charts. Crumple a nautical chart in your fist, Commander; give it creases like convolutions of a brain, and you can squeeze it into a very small container. Now carry the analogy one step further: suppose you double the area of the chart, refine it, thin its substance to tissue-paper thinness; then you can compress it into a container only slightly larger. You have now what appears to be a perfectly normal container, namely, the skull; but it contains something quite beyond the bounds of normality, namely, a double-sized brain. Something like this is believed to have occurred in the brains of The Intruders: they have twice the thinking surface of men, but their craniums are deceptively similar, only very slightly larger if at all."

Other "Intruders" had appeared in the long, long evolutionary history of Man, he said.

"The first hominoid of which we have any knowledge, the South African Plesianthropos, had a brain with a thinking area of 600 square centimeters. Then came Sinanthropus with 1200. Then modern man, like you and me, with 2400. There is nothing in between. It is not a slow growth. It is a series of double jumps: 600, 1200, 2400. Something caused those jumps; we do not know what, but it must have been unprecedented at the time, something impressed from without upon the organism. And now there is the figure of 4800 in beings like your son."

I said, "This has never been publicized. There have been, then, other deaths, other measurements, other autopsies?"

There had been a few, he said, mostly accident cases over a period of years; but they had not caused concern; nor had they been seriously studied at first. Here and there some child would drown or be run over by a car; later it would be discovered that the child had been unusually brilliant.

"Then they were studied. Statistics are mounting and researchers are beginning to fear that a totally new species of man, Homo Supersapiens, has suddenly appeared among us. They are believed to be relatively few in numbers. There were none before the Twenty Minute War and there is no record of one being born thereafter. Study of the exact time of their birth, where the records were not destroyed, indicates that they were all born at the precise moment of the detonation of the rockets that destroyed the Isthmus of Panama and were subjected to a millisecond of unknown radiation while the white light glared. Something in that light changed them. It did not change the mothers, so far as is known, though they must of course be watched. It did not change the fathers, subject to the same study. Indeed, the time lapse between conception and birth would seem to totally exonerate the parents. The Intruders are not therefore the result of a doubling of genes, as is the case in some of the X-ray-induced tetraploid flowers. Rather we believe that we shall find evidence of actual creation of matter in the crania of certain susceptible infants born at just that moment. It has long been know that matter can be converted into energy. That is what went into the bombs of the War. It is less well known, though frequently documented, that the reverse is also true and has been practically demonstrated not once but many times, namely, that energy can produce matter. We are looking for this in the brains of The Intruders. We think

some intrusion of instantly created matter lodged therein
and acted like a catalyst to vitalize the whole. That is what
we think, but we do not know. That is what sets them apart.
That is what has changed them and why we must fight them
to survive."

"It changed them for the better," I said miserably.

I thought of Angélique's fragile beauty. Owing to her
somewhat generous features, based, it had now been calibrated, on the somewhat large bone structure of her head, not
noticeable at first glance, her aristocratic beauty "carried"
like a lovely actress's across the footlights. Her mouth was
full and sensitive, verging indeed on the sensual but possess-
ing amazing mobility and capable of twisting into a contemptuous sneer when she observed anything that struck her
as ignoble, and her eyes were wide-spaced and limpid. She
had the features an actress tries to achieve with makeup,
but she had them naturally. Similarly, in a manly fashion, had
Bill.

The doctor now touched on the subject of eye pigmentation. "One of the clues we spot them by is the color of their
eyes. If they're blue we don't bother; they're people. If
they're brown, we don't know and we probe deeper; they're
suspect. Studies indicate that The Intruders never have blue
eyes. Evidence is growing that brown pigmentation provides
some sort of protection against deleterious effect of the
ultraviolet reaches of the spectrum, to which they are sensitive."

"I know. Like bees. Bill told me he could see the sun
through the clouds. It didn't save him, but he loved the
light."

"Not all of their sensitivities serve any useful purpose," he
said. "Some of them may actually be retrogressive, including
their queerly keen sense of smell. You and I detect odors less

acutely than an animal because we are civilized. They smell things like bloodhounds.

"Their sympathetic nervous system is oddly developed. This may account for their preternaturally swift muscular reactions."

I was not sure what the sympathetic nervous system was. He told me it was something like a brain in the backbone. We all have it. Lots of stimuli, he said, never reach the real brain. They go to the backbone and the body reacts, as it were, to a command from a closer signal-center. Much time is saved thereby, and the high thinking areas are relieved of the burden of conceptualizing purely repetitive mechanical functions and left more time to think. But this was a retrogressive phenomenon, he said, almost reptilian in character. The dinosaur had quite a swelling in his backbone for this very purpose. It didn't save the dinosaur. It was a drawback.

"We are working on weapons," he said, "to take full advantage of such failings as we ferret them out. It should be quite easy, for example, to blind The Intruders with cheaply produced UV projectors of sufficient power."

"Yes, I suppose you would do that," I said.

"Did your son ever mention the name of any of his friends who could also see like a bee?" the doctor said. "Anyone he happened to mention with UV vision."

He had in his hand a pencil, and he was doodling on a piece of paper, making little crosses. To me they looked like crosses in a graveyard.

"Only Angélique Bolduc," I said.

"Of course we caught her," he said.

"None of this would have happened if they had got to the airport in time to catch the plane to Kamchatka," Betty said.

The Commissioner said, smiling an unpleasant smile of triumph, "I think I ought to tell you, Mrs. Young, that the

Kamchatka plane met with an accident just after it took off. There was an explosion. The ten officials were killed along with the crew and a few of my men, some of whom had taken part in the execution of your son. They were in an emotional state and I thought it prudent to send them away for a while till they recovered their balance. They would also be less prone to gossip in Kamchatka."

It was clear to me that the murdered and the murderers had been ruthlessly disposed of in a buckshot blast of one planted bomb, guilty, suspect and innocent, all. One cannot accuse the Commissioner of inefficiency.

I was uncomfortably aware that Betty and I were privy to a critical secret. Our boy and the girl he wanted to marry, together with nine others like them, eleven in all, plus the executioners who hated them and could not be trusted to hold their tongues, plus who knew how many ordinary men of the crew, pawns in a game they knew naught of, had been blotted out in the secret war. I did not much care about myself, for I was sick at heart, but I was concerned for my wife.

So I said to the Commissioner, tailoring my response to the thing he wanted to hear, "It was good of you and the doctor to take so much time to explain all this to Mrs. Young and me. Without knowing the great issues at stake we might have gossiped, to the detriment of your work. It is clear that we have begotten a generation of vipers, and a man's foes shall be they of his own household, as the Bible says."

"I hoped you would feel that way, Commander," he said. "Above everything else we cannot afford loose tongues."

"You need have no fear on that score as far as we are concerned," I assured him. The fears were all on my side.

"We count on you both," he said pleasantly, rising and extending his hand, which I shook, looking away so as not to see the ghost of the blood I had begotten. On this we were dismissed.

I thought my Gethsemane was at an end. I thought I would be permitted to return home and pick up the disrupted pieces of my life and mourn my loss in dignity and privacy. I needed and expected the decent obscurity that society affords even to parents of hardened criminals who meet their end in the gas chamber; but this was denied me.

Recently I have been advised, through channels, that I am "permitted" to retire with the rank of Rear Admiral because of my services during the building of The Dam. Since many others contributed more than I, and I am not that old, I went at once to see Narcisse Bolduc. But he and his family have returned to the Gaspé, or so I was told.

When I did not immediately take advantage of the retirement offer my Admiral sent me a courier with a verbal message that I should do so at once. It is an order. No personal discretion is left me. I have known the Admiral for many years and I was incensed at his sudden formality. But no doubt he too had his orders. Betty says that there is a falling off in the calls she receives from our friends. We are avoided. There is a stigma on us. We do not know why. I have kept my word to the Commissioner. Neither by direct statement nor by oblique implication have I or my wife ever hinted that there was anything unusual about our son's death. We have cleaved to the terse announcement subsequently published by his employer that he died of natural causes while engaged in an obscure construction project in a distant locality. There are many of these new places, all with new names. There is no better way of burying an obituary or a murdered son.

The Commissioner did indeed do me the honor of permitting me to see Bill's coffin, but sealed and under guard.

I asked the guard to open it, hoping to erase from my memory the picture of his battered face and the red-soaked sheet, trusting in the skill of the embalmer to have eliminated the worst of the outward signs of violence. But the guard said unpleasantly, "My orders are to keep it closed." I could not escape the suspicion that, after the extensive autopsy, there was nothing left that I would have recognized as Wilson Young, Jr. I did not demur, knowing that I was watched and for fear of retaliation by the Commissioner. The whole authority of the fighting world in which I have always been proud to play some small part has united to will him out of existence, indeed out of memory or mention, Bill and all his kind. Perhaps this is best. Surely it is best. We must survive, and not as brainless helots. Fortunately their number is thought to be few, and they become fewer as we forge ahead in the war for survival against them.

Sometimes on the street I experience an uneasy feeling that I am being watched, and when I look around a pair of clear, cold eyes, heart-breakingly like Bill's, is fixed upon me, and then some handsome young person will slip away and disappear into the crowd. They are growing older; they are more clever at hiding their peculiarities; they act more like people. They are maturing, reaching toward their prime and their awful potential. I have of course dutifully reported every instance of this sort to the Commissioner, and I have no doubt that appropriate action has been taken.

It would be pleasant but unrealistic to hope that we and our gifted offspring, for they are our own, could live peaceably side by side and that our civilization could reap the vast benefits of their wonderful powers. Heaven would bend down very close to earth, as I think, if they represented salvation instead of a dire threat to our poor old planet, so recently snatched from a mortal illness; admittedly of our making but also of our curing. They will not have it so. No more, I suppose, would we have the Tasmanians.

But instinctive reaction against them, a feeling I share, is so primitive and violent that I cannot be optimistic. No course is open to us but to eliminate them, whenever and wherever we can spot them.

I shall always retain a great sympathy, nay, more than that, a reverence for the enemy, remembering Bill; but I shall not be on their side, remembering the savage Tasmanians, too stupid to live, and further back, as the anthropologists teach us, the still more savage, still more stupid Neanderthal Man, poor soul, if he had one.

❋ ❋ ❋ ❋ ❋

Today there occurred a damned annoying thing. I am ordered north by reason of my severance from the Service. I never asked for retirement, but it has come. My replacement will take over my house here. The Admiral informs me that my wife and I will be given permanent retirement quarters in New Chicago, bigger and more suitable for a rear admiral's rank, and that I can feel free at any time to volunteer to the Lake Authorities for any job that interests me in all the lacustrine reconstruction up there, so at least I shall not be idle. I asked if that meant the Seaway too. He said why not try. Well, at least I am not to be beached and relegated to paltry inspection jobs that a twenty-year-old midshipman could handle. [Note: The last twelve words of this sentence were heavily scored out by Admiral Young, but legible after processing.]

I shall no longer have a view of the sea and the beautiful structure I helped to build, but I am promised a view of Lake Michigan, now all blue water again. This is a great consolation.

I deeply regret the necessity of destroying these pages, but there is no doubt that I must. I suspect that the Commissioner still has me under surveillance, though I have observed no evidence of it lately. But the sire of an Intruder never really feels safe. So I will burn these pages and cast them upon the wind. They have served their purpose. They have afforded me solace at a most trying period of my personal life, a solace I could not have achieved in any other fashion. But now I am ordered north. I shall take a ship, of course. Ships have been my life. Some damned prying Lake Inspector at the end of the line is sure to go through my possessions, and the more cleverly I try to hide this, my tribute to my son, the more certain some rascal is, whoever he may be, through my own bad luck and stupidity, to find it, since I never seem able to outwit the other fellow. Worse, it might fall into wrong hands, namely, The Intruders'. You never quite know whom you're dealing with. That would be a monstrous betrayal of my kind. There is a beautiful French word, "adieu." It means, "farewell." It also means, way back when it started, "To God": that is to say, "I commit you to God and His mercy," very much compacted. Bill taught me that. So, Bill, my son, my son, *adieu.*

A FOOTNOTE: to be docketed for general reference if, hopefully, our numbers increase to the point where we win.

It goes without saying that Rear Admiral and Mrs. Young never reached New Chicago. The Commissioner's cynical surveillance, a revealing facet of their mentality, made sure of that. Their ship is officially registered in the World Chiefs' roster as having foundered in a gale. We have evidence that it was brutally bombed, and no survivors were permitted to escape.

As for the Admiral's narrative of the War, it affords a clue, when added to others which we are gathering, to how they think, and a full minute is recommended the student of anthropology with a bent towards the ethos of the primitives, for its absorption, fixation and review.

The manner of its salvage may be deemed of interest, since the following matter could not of necessity be included in the Admiral's text:

He did indeed burn the pages, but he did not "cast them upon the wind." He seems to have been a tidy soul, a product of their military mind; and he would have disliked so many ashes. He put them in a wax paper bag and he walked towards the sea, apprehensive also, no doubt, of the prohibition against burning trash which was still in effect, the nuclei of ashes having been a contributory factor in the formation of The Big Ice and, as they thought, a hazard of its return.

Once arrived at the beach he lifted the bag and made a tentative gesture as if to hurl it into the sea. But he saw children swimming close by, and one may speculate that he hesitated to shower them with ashes, which might get into and cause pain in the eyes of those who could not see them coming, correctly assuming that the bag might disintegrate in the air. Many of them are extraordinarily kind to children though savage amongst their mature homogeny. Whatever his motivation, the writer of this footnote observed that he paused in the typical abulic indecision that characterizes their better specimens, as opposed to the violence that characterizes their worst, and, spotting me, swimming vigorously, shouted, "Hey, kid!"

I recognized him at once by the usual signs as a putative co-progenitor and hence deserving of the thirty-year one-generation immunity; and, holding myself severely in check, made a great show of hastening to the shore, splashing and fumbling with simulated lack of coordination and cried out, "Yes, sir?"

"You swim mighty fine," said the Admiral. "Want to earn a pocket full of credits?"

"Oh, yes, sir."

But I forgot to change my voice. The Admiral said sharply, "How old are you?"

"Thirteen, sir," I piped, coughing and spitting as if an intake of salt water had affected my vocal apparatus and speaking in a high childish treble. I could not, for obvious reasons, reveal my real age.

"Careful," said Admiral Young. "Don't swallow too much of that. It'll dehydrate you."

You could not help liking him.

"It'll what?"

"Never mind, son. You'll learn about that when you grow up. See this?"

The Admiral pointed to the wax paper bag in his hand.

"See what, sir?"

"This bag, you idiot. See it?"

"Oh that. Oh, yes, sir. It's a bag."

"And how heavy is it, do you think?"

Adopting the Admiral's phraseology, I answered, "Heck, mister, I dunno. Maybe ten pounds. It looks pretty big."

"How far could you swim with ten pounds?"

"Golly, maybe a hundred yards."

"Well, it weighs, I should say, ten ounces. How far could you swim with ten ounces if you could swim a hundred yards with ten pounds?"

"Golly, I dunno." I sensed it would be unkind to give the simple answer. The putative co-progenitor would have been hurt in his pride to no purpose.

"That is the trouble with kids nowadays," the Admiral

sighed, and he hurled the bag at me. I caught it with ease but I made it look clumsy. The Admiral was woefully wide of the mark.

"Now swim out as far as you can," the Admiral said, "bearing in mind that you've got to swim back again. Don't drown, boy. Take no chances. That's how I always got along."

"Yes, sir," I said.

"And rip the bag to pieces and let it disintegrate in the water." He tossed me a hundred-credit coin. "OK?"

"OK," I said, and swam out and out and out while the Admiral trudged his weary way up the dunes and disappeared in the direction of the ship that would take him north to his death.

We reconstituted the ashes into the Admiral's original text by a simple elaboration of the gum-linen-backing method by which they themselves had reconstituted the Dead Sea Scrolls. We have learned so much from them.

It is painful to find reference again and again in the Admiral's text that we are cold and unfeeling.

When we win they will know what we are, poor self-destroying remnant of the helots. But they were a mighty race.